"DO YOU REMEMBER THIS FEELING, DEE?" MATT asked, his hands caressing her back through the soft cashmere.

"Yes," she gasped involuntarily at the sensations that surged through her. He stroked her cheek, then ran the edge of his nail along her bottom lip. She was desperate to taste him, but he barely brushed her lips with his, back and forth.

"Matt, kiss me!" Dee cried out in frustration.

He laughed softly into her hair and cradled her tighter against him. "Just like in school. I couldn't then, the housemother turned on the lights. I had to leave . . ."

"But you came back," Dee finished.

"Yes." He grinned. "And it was like this . . ." He showed her how well he remembered, running his lips down her neck to her collarbone. Then he drew her fingers into his mouth one by one until she was weak and breathless, yearning for more. "Matt . . . Matt . . ." she sighed, begging for the kisses with which he'd wooed her.

"Soon. Wait for it, Dee. Feel the need building. Experience everything with me, the way it was—the way it will always be with us. . . ."

WHAT ARE *LOVESWEPT* ROMANCES?

They are stories of true romance and touching emotion. We believe those two very important ingredients are constants in our highly sensual and very believable stories in the LOVESWEPT line. Our goal is to give you, the reader, stories of consistently high quality that may sometimes make you laugh, sometimes make you cry, but are always fresh and creative and contain many delightful surprises within their pages.

Most romance fans read an enormous number of books. Those they truly love, they keep. Others may be traded with friends and soon forgotten. We hope that each LOVESWEPT romance will be a treasure—a "keeper." We will always try to publish

LOVE STORIES YOU'LL NEVER FORGET
BY AUTHORS YOU'LL ALWAYS REMEMBER

The Editors

Loveswept ® 645

SHEER DELIGHT

JUDY GILL

BANTAM BOOKS

NEW YORK · TORONTO · LONDON · SYDNEY · AUCKLAND

SHEER DELIGHT
A Bantam Book / October 1993

LOVESWEPT® *and the wave design are registered
trademarks of Bantam Books, a division of
Bantam Doubleday Dell Publishing Group, Inc.
Registered in U.S. Patent
and Trademark Office and elsewhere.*

*If you would be interested in receiving protective vinyl covers for your
Loveswept books, please write to this address for information:*

Loveswept
Bantam Books
P.O. Box 985
Hicksville, NY 11802

ISBN 0-553-44262-7

Published simultaneously in the United States and Canada

Bantam Books are published by Bantam Books, a division of Bantam Doubleday Dell Publishing Group, Inc. Its trademark, consisting of the words
"Bantam Books" and the portrayal of a rooster, is Registered in U.S. Patent
and Trademark Office and in other countries. Marca Registrada. Bantam
Books, 1540 Broadway, New York, New York 10036.

PRINTED IN THE UNITED STATES OF AMERICA

OPM   0 9 8 7 6 5 4 3 2 1

ONE

It not only looked erotic, it smelled that way, too, spicy and exotic and musky. Matt Fiedler obeyed the impulse that had brought him to the edge of the open doorway. Hesitating only a moment, he stepped farther inside, activating a set of delicate Oriental chimes.

He took two short paces forward. A thick carpet, the same soft gray color of the walls, muffled his footfalls as the chiming faded. Decorating accents of peachy pink and pale green created a distinctly feminine atmosphere. He stood still, moving only his eyes as he accustomed himself to the unfamiliar ambience of a ladies' lingerie store.

Sheer Delight, the name on the window had said. It was one of five stores located on the ground floor of the Westmarch Apartment Hotel.

That name, conjuring up evocative images, had drawn him into the boutique. He'd intended to do a walk-around of the building on which Metcom, Inc., his employer, had a purchase option. Then, seeing a silk teddy displayed in the glass showcase set into the building's outer wall, he had decided to investigate. The teddy was black, trimmed with the palest of pink lace, and sheer, as the store's name implied, and undoubtedly would be a delight if seen on the right woman.

If he were an adman, rather than corporate trouble-shooter, it was a name he might have come up with, he thought. The person who had named the place had a mind on the same wavelength as his.

He took another slow step into the store, reached out, and touched a flowing white negligee, feeling the heavy satin under his fingertips, the softness of the marabou feathers brush over his wrist.

"Good morning."

He jumped at the sound of the voice and snatched his hand away from the white satin negligee, feeling vaguely ashamed, as if he'd been caught going through a woman's closet.

"May I help you, or would you like to browse a little longer?"

That voice! At the sound of it every hair on his body stood erect. He whirled and stared. All he could see of the woman was one eye, one eyebrow, a sweep of smooth chestnut hair, and a slender forearm and hand with golden-tan skin. But the back of his neck prickled, and his mouth went suddenly dry.

It couldn't be. No. He was hallucinating. "That's all right," he said. "I was just leav—"

"Matt?" The interruption cut his words. It came as a squeak of sound as she dropped the boxes to the counter, staring at him from wide bright blue eyes. "Matt?" she said again, coming out from behind the counter. It was a whisper of shocked disbelief. She took another step forward, paused, blinked, and said his name again triumphantly, as if she'd just created him. "Matt!"

Dee was not responsible for the irrepressible smile that spread across her face. She felt it glowing through her entire body. "Matt Fielder!" she said. It *was* him. He was older, of course, broader in the shoulders, wearing not the jeans and T-shirt college uniform she remembered, but a fawn raincoat over a dark blue three-piece suit. His dark hair, beaded now with rain, had been expertly styled. Once he had simply allowed it to grow until it got in the way, then hacked some of it off in the bathroom. But he was still Matt.

Reaching him, she put out her hands in greeting. "Well, look at you! You've scarcely changed in, let's see—what must it be?—twelve, fifteen years?"

"Thirteen," he said, taking her hands and smiling down at her. He looked as stunned and bemused as she felt.

His hands engulfed hers in a way that her body remembered instantly and in poignant detail. Thirteen years. Oh, yes, she knew that, all right. She hadn't needed him to tell her exactly how long it had been. Thirteen years, five-and-one-half months—six, come the first of December. She gazed at him, up into those same hazel eyes that had once been the center of her universe.

Thirteen years. Lord, but a lot of tides had come in and out since then.

"It's good to see you again." It was. She was not merely observing the social graces. Her head reeled with a foolish, giddy thrill at seeing him looking so tall, so strong, and virile. Oh, good heavens! Had she learned nothing in thirteen years? She tried to withdraw, to step back, but he held her hands firmly, not letting her go. She retreated emotionally, putting herself at a distance she knew she must maintain.

This man had walked out on her. He had betrayed her trust in him. He had broken her heart. And what was she doing? Wagging and wriggling like a lost puppy returned to its master?

Where was her pride?

Her tone cooled several degrees to the level it should have been in the beginning as she said, "How are you, Matt?"

"I'm fine." He rubbed the pads of his thumbs over her knuckles, and this time she managed to break free. Quickly, she tucked her hands behind her back, linking them tightly out of sight of those eyes she had once known to be all-seeing. She had no reason to tremble. Yet tremble she did.

"And you," he said, his eyes crinkling in a network of laugh lines that had only been hinted at when he was twenty-three. "You've certainly changed, Dee. I hadn't thought you could be improved upon." He took in her shape, clearly outlined, she knew, by the fine knit of her soft rose-colored wool dress. "You grew up"—He cleared his throat and went on—"real . . . really beautiful, kid."

"'Kid,'" she said, her voice coming out all husky and choked again when she wanted cool and remote. "I can't remember the last time anyone called me that." Of course she could. He was the last—the only—person to have called her that. It was as close to an endearment as he'd ever come. He'd called her "duchess" at times, but as a gentle insult, reproof for what he considered haughtiness. "But I'm no longer nineteen, Matt."

His gaze swept over her again, lingering here and there. "I know." He swallowed visibly. "I can see that."

"What . . . what are you doing here?" she asked. All Matt seemed capable of doing was looking at her in a manner that made her distinctly uncomfortable.

Her question troubled him, she could see. Then his mouth quirked into that funny little crooked grin she discovered could still make her insides lurch. He hedged. "You mean here as on the West Coast, here as in this building, or here"—with a low, bemused chuckle, he glanced around as if he couldn't quite believe his surroundings—"as in this shop?"

That laugh was just as she remembered, deep, sexy,

and throaty, as if he were coming down with a cold. It had always made her want to mother him, make him well again. Only the Matt of those days had been too tough, too stubborn, to get sick, or to admit to needing anyone. He'd been moving too fast to get caught by a germ.

Or by a woman.

She wondered if he'd slowed down at all.

"Well . . . any of those," she said lightly. "Or all. Are you on the coast for business? And are you here, in my store, looking for something to take home to your wife?"

"I'm in town on business, was walking past the building, and I came into the store on impulse. I'm not married." Matt was struck suddenly by the relief he felt in being able to say that to Dee. It came almost as a sense of having had a lucky escape. He wished he could see her hand to check for rings, but she'd shoved them both behind her back. He could tell by the rigidity of her shoulders that she had her fists clenched together the way she'd used to do when she was nervous.

Was she nervous now? About him? If so, why? Possible answers sent his heart racing crazily.

"Are you?" he asked.

"Married?" His eyes narrowed in response to the snooty tilt of her chin. "No." *And what gives you the right to ask?* she didn't say. She didn't have to.

For a moment his temper threatened to rise. *Who the hell has a better right?* he wanted to ask, but of course he couldn't. Thirteen years ago he'd walked out on this woman, broken a promise to return, even if it had been one she'd forced out of him. As he had made it, he'd known it was one he must break. But he'd been a coward when it came to Dee, had taken the easy way out, promised, then not returned.

He glanced around again, desperately seeking a safe topic for discussion, suddenly more ill at ease than he'd been since his first job interview. "So, this is your, um, store?"

She brought her hands out from behind her back in a sweeping, possessive gesture, filled with pride. "One of them, yes."

"You have more than one?"

"Three," Dee said, watching Matt's eyes carefully as she spoke. "Though this was the first one, and the one where I have my business office. We've been here for nearly five years. We opened Sheer Delight Two in West Vancouver a couple of years ago, and Sheer Delight Three in Oakridge last June."

He showed no signs of distress at learning she was a successful businesswoman, and she felt an odd sense of relief. Which was, she told herself, quite foolish. Meeting Matt again was a chance occurrence. He would no more concern himself over her personal success now than he would over the success of the holding company she owned along with her mother. Not that she had anything to do with Embassy Holdings or could take any credit for its prosperity, but it might . . . intimidate Matt.

She smiled. Matt didn't look as if he could be intimidated. But then, he never had.

"Well, now," she said when he remained silent. "What can I help you with, Matt? Or would you care to browse?"

"I . . . uh, I told you, I wasn't here to buy." Had he told her that? "It—it was the name that drew me in. Intrigued me. Sheer Delight. How did you arrive at that?"

Her wide-eyed gaze fixed on his face, she said, "I thought you'd have made the connection at once, seeing me here."

"Connec—Oh! Of course. Delight." He grinned. "You know, I'd clean forgotten that your name is Delight. I simply remembered you as Dee."

Those clear blue eyes looked up into his, candid, questioning. Her smile had gone.

"Did you really?" she asked as if it scarcely mattered to her, or as if it amused her that he would bother to say it. "Remember me, I mean? At other times, or just when you walked in here and saw me?"

He had to clear his throat again before he could reply. "I remembered, Dee. Every now and then I'd see a head of dark reddish-brown hair shining in the sun, and I'd remember. Or I'd catch a glimpse of a profile that could have been yours." He smiled. "Or hear a regal tone, an imperious turn of phrase, and look quickly to see if it was you."

He obeyed an impulse that came from somewhere very deep inside and lifted a hand, stroking one finger down the curve of her face. "I've thought about you." Her skin was as smooth as the satin of the gown he had fingered. He remembered that it had been that way all over her body. He suddenly pictured her in one of those sexy little items showcased against the walls. And responded to it in a very red-blooded male way. "A man never forgets his first love."

Dee's knees went weak at the touch of his finger on her cheek. And neither did a woman forget her first love. Her first lover. Even one who had hurt her as badly as Matt had. Goose bumps pricked the skin of her arms. She tugged the sleeves of her dress down from her elbows to her wrists.

Oh, Lord! This couldn't be happening. She couldn't possibly be responding to Matt Fiedler. Not again. She knew better now. She knew the penalties for forgetting the lessons life had taught her. Lessons he had, as a once-vital part of her life, helped her to learn.

"And you?" he asked. "Did you remember me?"

She laughed and slipped away from him, back behind the counter where she felt safer. "Of course. Every time I saw a horror movie on TV."

He followed her and leaned his arms one on either side of the stack of boxes she half hid behind, laughing at her over the top of them. "That, Ms. Farris, does not sound like a compliment. What reminded you most of me? *The Blob? The Fly?*"

"*Godzilla,*" she said. She pulled the top box out from under his chin and withdrew a slip, gave it a shake, and hung it on the rack of padded hangers behind the counter. She squirted a jet of warm steam over it, and the creases fell away. "Or maybe it was *King Kong.*"

His eyes danced, and she wished she hadn't made the comparison. She though of the dark mat of hair on his chest and stomach, the coarse hair on his legs and arms, recalling how it had tickled her body.

"Hey! Come on," he said reproachfully. "*King Kong* was no horror movie."

She steamed another slip. "It scared me."

Matt lifted the next one from the box and held it by thin straps of satin ribbon. His large hand looked even larger, even tanner, handling the delicate garment.

"Pretty," he said. "Do you do all the buying for your stores?"

She didn't meet his gaze. "Yes."

She worked quickly to hang the lingerie, working through the green, then beginning on a box of blue. Though this was not her personal apparel, it made her uncomfortable for Matt to watch her handling it, for him to be touching it, too, lifting things and admiring them, passing them to her to hang. It was much too intimate. He didn't belong in her store. He was too masculine. Too much. And he certainly didn't belong in her life.

As if sensing her anxieties, he shoved his hands into the pockets of his raincoat, leaving her to the unpacking.

His grin caught her full force as she glanced at him. "I remember how all the horror movies we saw together scared you," he said. "You're the only girl who ever curled up on my lap so I could protect her from demons and ghosts. Remember *It's Alive?*"

"Oh! Yes." For a moment her hands stilled within the folds of pale aqua silk. She did remember the film. But what she remembered most was the feel of his hard chest, his encircling arms, his thighs under her. The scent of his skin. All of that had made his favorite scary films worth watching. Quickly, she banished the memories and steamed the slip.

He grinned wickedly. "And how about *The Shining?*"

"Lordy, yes! 'Redrum!'" They laughed together for a moment. It was far too easy to laugh with Matt. She should be ordering him out. "That word still makes me shudder," she said.

He laughed again, and his eyes crinkled, speaking to her silently. Deeper grooves bracketed his mouth. Good heavens but maturity became him. He'd never been a handsome man, never would be, but something about him had always been able to set her senses on fire.

It surely had a lot to do with that almost indefinable expression in his eyes, she thought, a built-in, basically reckless attitude, a Let's-do-it-I-dare-you look, combined with a cocky assurance of his own ability to get away with things, to arouse responses. And to please.

He certainly hadn't lost any of it.

His gaze followed her hands as she folded tissue paper and laid it aside. Then he asked softly, "And do you still watch horror movies curled up in someone's lap?"

Dee opened another box. "No," she said, slipping yellow satin ribbon straps onto a hanger. "I don't watch horror movies at all."

"What do you watch? And with whom?"

"Not much," she said, choosing to ignore the second question. "Running a business leaves me little time for entertainment." Besides, horror movies were not something to watch alone. And since Gavin, she'd been mostly that way.

"What do you do, Matt?" It was time to turn this conversation around. "And where do you live? Did you complete law school as you intended? Are you out there defending the defenseless and fighting oppression wherever you find it?"

His expression darkened as he stood erect, half turning from her to look out into the cobblestoned courtyard where cold November rain slanted down. "No," he said.

She winced. Dead dreams. She could see them in his profile, in the harshness of his mouth, the set of his jaw. She wished she hadn't asked her question so flippantly. What had happened to dim his visions? She'd never once considered that maybe he hadn't come back to her because he couldn't. . . .

"I have a law degree. I'm a troubleshooter and point man for a development company. In Toronto."

"That must be . . . interesting," she said, beginning on a box of lacy bra-and-panty sets while his attention was elsewhere.

He glanced back at her. "It's varied," he allowed. He looked at the underwear in her hand, then at her breasts, her hips, as if envisioning her in the garments. She knew the second he became aware that she'd noticed the direction of his stare. His eyes flickered with greenish lights. Not quite laughing. At her? At himself?

"Maybe it isn't as exciting or as emotionally rewarding as the kind of law I once dreamed of practicing," he said, "but reality is something everyone has to face. And the rewards are . . . the kind I needed. Financial. Student loans have to be repaid, and real life happens to even the most idealistic."

She nodded as she finished with the bras and panties and wheeled the filled rack out into the store. "I understand that." Real life had happened for her when Matt had failed to return to McGill University that long-ago September. Maybe it had happened even before that, when he'd refused to take her with him when he'd been called home to Nova Scotia that summer. But . . . it *had* been a long time ago. Recriminations were no longer in order.

She began transferring the garments to their different departments.

He followed her, long legs moving lithely. In his fawn- colored knee-length trench coat he reminded her of a stalking cougar. His cocked eyebrow, the twist of his mouth, told her he doubted that she did understand.

Dee slapped a hanger onto a rack with unnecessary force. All right, so she hadn't required student loans. But having rich parents hadn't meant she'd had to work less hard for her grades, or that she was incapable of empathizing with her friends who had had to work their way through college to supplement their scholarships and loans.

"By the look of things," Matt said, "you changed your mind about the direction of your life too. You're not exactly out there in the real world writing daring journalistic exposés of those same oppressors against whom I was going to defend the defenseless."

"That's right. Once, I did. But now I'm a shopkeeper."

As if the curtness of her reply had told him more than she'd intended, his expression, his tone, gentled as he said, "What happened, kid?"

To his dismay Matt saw a shadow flit across Dee's eyes, eyes that should never be filled with anything but sunshine and smiles. "It's a long story," she said.

He put a hand on her shoulder, feeling the delicacy of her bones through her dress. She'd always been fragile.

The sudden surge of protectiveness that ripped through him nearly sent him to his knees. Could he ever make her understand? Would she even want to at this late date?

"I have time, Dee," he said, mentally cursing the ragged note in his voice. What he wanted was cool sophistication, the kind she'd been born with, the kind he thought he'd finally developed. Why had it deserted him now?

"My next meeting's not till two." He couldn't think of a better place to spend the intervening hours than in this boutique with its dainty, beautiful garments and its inviting, erotic aroma.

Or a better person to be with than Dee Farris.

He hadn't felt that way about any place, or any person, for a long, long time.

"Tell me about your life," he said.

"I—" She broke off and bit her lip, and he was struck by the sadness in her eyes before she slid her gaze away. She shook her head. Her relief, as three women came through the entrance, was almost palpable.

Matt stopped her as she would have gone forward to offer assistance. "Can we continue this reunion over lunch?" he asked quietly.

She shook her head as she pulled her arm free. "I won't be taking a lunch break today. My assistant isn't in."

"If not lunch, then dinner," he persisted.

Dee shook her head. Even through the fabric of her dress, his touch had sent a welter of sensations over her skin, scary sensations, unnecessary ones. They couldn't be allowed to recur. She gave him an easy smile but no explanation. She'd learned long ago that it wasn't required. "I'm sorry, Matt, but no."

He wasn't going to let her get away with that. She should have known, remembered. "Why not?" he asked, his jaw squaring up determinedly, his dark brows lowering over his hazel eyes.

Tilting her chin, maintaining her smile, she nevertheless managed to cool her voice considerably, while still sounding friendly. "Because I don't care to have dinner with you."

That should have been the end of it. It would have been if he'd been any other man. This was, after all, the nineties. A woman had as much right to say no as she had to say yes.

His eyes glittered behind his thick lashes. "And why not, might I ask, duchess? Is there a man in your life who'd object?" His tone was as coolly pleasant as hers had been. His smile committed blatant falsehoods. "If so, he's invited too." That, too, was a lie.

She glanced at her customers. They seemed content to browse and chat among themselves. "There is no man in my life at present," she said.

His smile flickered, then turned warm and genuine, reflecting in his eyes. "Fine. Then there is no reason why we shouldn't dine together and catch up on each other's lives."

There was every reason. The prime one being that she wanted desperately to say yes. Another good reason to say no was that the same things about him that had attracted her when she'd been a girl worked even better now that she was a woman. But she was a woman who had made a life for herself, a woman who liked that life and wasn't looking to change it.

Besides, he had clearly come into her store with the intention of buying something for someone. A man didn't normally pick up filmy, madly expensive lingerie for his mother or his sister. And Matt, she knew, had neither.

No, he might not be married, but there was obviously a woman in his life.

Since that was the case, Dee wasn't biting. Having been hurt that way herself, she refused to risk another woman's peace of mind and happiness.

"Matt," she said, "believe me, it's been nice, very nice, seeing you again. But up till about fifteen minutes ago you had no more idea that I lived in Vancouver than I had that you might pop into this store between business sessions. We may have known each other long ago, but that doesn't mean we have anything in common anymore. We've both done perfectly well without each other for thirteen years. There's no reason we can't continue to do so. So let's not try to make more of it than it really is."

"I'm not making more of it than that," he said. He touched the pulse in her throat, drawing her attention to the rapidity of it. And to his knowledge of it. "Are you?"

Heat flared through her, and she jerked away. "Of course not!"

"Then why not have dinner with me tonight and prove to me that we have nothing in common? After all, old friends do things like that every day. What will it cost you? A few hours of time, maybe a little boredom once we dispose of 'Do you remember so-and-so?' and 'What ever happened to her?' But then you can go your way and I can go mine, and no one's hurt. So, why not?"

She drew in a deep breath. Why not indeed? When he put it like that, it seemed completely innocent. The memory of his thumb pressing against the telltale pulse in her throat suggested that if she refused, he'd go away thinking she was frightened by what he might be able to stir up.

But if she accepted, there was a distinct possibility that he'd touch her again.

And then he'd know for sure.

At any rate, no matter which option she took, she knew he'd go away again. Probably, despite his denial, with some sexy undergarment for the lady in his life.

And that being the case, as he said, why not? It was a long time since she'd had dinner with a charming man. And she knew beyond any doubt that once all the "remember whens" were out of the way, boredom would not be a problem. Not with Matt across the table. As for his lady, she couldn't possibly be hurt by Matt's having dinner with someone he himself described as "an old friend." Not when that old friend had no intention of enjoying anything more than good food and pleasant conversation.

"All right." She capitulated with a smile she hoped came across as nonchalant and jaunty. "When and where? I'll meet you."

He laughed softly, a deep rumble that attracted the attention of the three customers, all of whom looked him over in clear appreciation. "Don't you remember even the basics about me?" he asked. "I can see it's time we had another date, if for no other reason than to remind you of the way I operate, as old-fashioned as it may seem. I pick up my date at her door, Dee. And I return her to it."

His hard look said he'd accept no argument. "Give me your address."

She realized as she finished explaining that she rented an apartment in the building that she shouldn't feel such astonishment at having caved in so easily. Matt had always had a way of getting what he wanted. He smiled. Once more he touched her cheek. "Tonight," he said very quietly. "At eight."

By tonight, Dee swore, she'd find the strength to show him that he couldn't always have his own way.

Tonight. At eight.

The thought sent delicious bubbles of excitement fluttering through her veins.

TWO

This time Matt entered the stately old building fronting on English Bay through the residential entrance. He strolled up a flight of marble stairs from the street below, under a green-and-white-striped canopy, and a uniformed doorman swung wide a set of gilt-lettered beveled-glass doors. He asked Matt's name, ushered him toward the back of a lobby smelling of antiquity and lemon oil, and spoke deferentially into an intercom. "Mr. Fiedler has arrived, Miss Farris."

Dee's disembodied voice came through clearly. "Fine, Jenkins. You may send him up." He used a key to open the doors to a walnut-paneled elevator and admitted Matt. There were no numbers, Matt's first indication as to what he might find at the top of his ascent. The elevator rose slowly, then eased to a stop. He stepped out into the unexpected environment of a warm, moist solarium.

Intrigued, he stopped and stared around at the sweeping palms, bright tropical flowers, and climbing vines illuminated by strategically placed lights. Several small birds twittered and fluttered in the branches of a tree at the right of the elevator, then took off in a cloud of yellow and black. Water trickled down a rocky spillway and splashed into a pool.

A scarlet macaw swooped toward him, then angled away to land on the branch of a broad-leafed tree, shrieking.

As if the macaw's scream had been a signal, Dee appeared from behind a fan-shaped palm. She wore a long, loose cotton garment and a pair of gardening gloves. In one hand she carried a basket of firm bright red tomatoes.

"Hello, Matt," she said. For just an instant he was sure he detected excitement in her blue eyes. Then, with a cool, polite smile, she asked, "Well? What do you think of my front porch?"

"I'm . . . amazed," he said. "It's unique, as front porches go. That is, compared to the front porches of my past experience."

But then, his past experiences and hers had never exactly been on a par.

Dee, her unexpected "front porch," and even the building itself spoke of old, solid money, and he experienced what could only be a rapid emotional time trip backward. It tumbled him into momentary despair. He struggled to overcome it.

Why did he feel somehow betrayed by finding her there in those circumstances? He had known them almost, but not quite, from the beginning. Had he known them at the very first, there would have been no "beginning" for them.

He thought of what her lease for this penthouse must cost and wondered why she hadn't simply bought the entire building long ago rather than risk losing not only her business premises but a home she clearly loved and cared for. He was certain that the solarium hadn't existed until Dee had created it.

"String beans," she said, tipping the basket so he could see into the bottom of it. "I'm experimenting with South African gem squash as well, but it's not bearing fruit yet. I also grow other salad vegetables, like lettuce and cucumbers, radishes and green onions."

Matt laughed. "I'm impressed."

Dee smiled. "You are not. I'm sorry. Hydroponic gardening is a hobby of mine, but I know most other people couldn't care less, so you don't need to be polite about it. Come in. I just have to get my shoes and coat."

She disappeared again around the fan palm, and he followed, stepping through a curtain of bamboo beads that rattled as it settled behind him, blocking the flight of the macaw, which had swooped again, still curious about the intruder.

Dee awaited him in the foyer that separated her apartment proper from the solarium. The basket of vegetables sat on a small, round table with fluted edges that undoubtedly was a priceless antique. She had shed the duster and gloves and stepped into a pair of black high heels.

The light shimmered on her hair and put a glow in her cheeks. The skin of her arms and shoulders, seen through the lace bolero she wore over a strapless black satin sheath, tempted his hands almost unbearably. The diamond studs in her earlobes caught the gleaming of the crystal drops of the small chandelier overhead.

"Dee . . ." He tried to swallow the roughness in his throat. "You look stunning," he said hoarsely. Now, he truly was impressed.

She stepped back another pace, and her correct little smile never faltered. "Thank you, Matt," she said ever so politely. The quintessential diplomat's daughter. She reached into a closet near the door and took out a black wool coat with a high pale fur collar. "Shall we go?"

"You're all ready?" He couldn't help sounding surprised.

She arched her fine brows. "You said eight, didn't you?"

"Yes, but I always figure in the lost-earring factor. Our dinner reservation isn't until eight-forty-five." He had also hoped to be invited in for a drink.

"You reminded me of the basics about you. Have you

forgotten that I've always prided myself on my punctuality?"

"Yes," he said, astonished that he actually had forgotten that detail about her. "I guess I'm no longer accustomed to punctual women."

She smiled with a hint of pride. "I'm always on time, and I never lose my earrings."

He nodded, feeling as if he'd been chastised, and took her coat, sliding it on for her. The fur framed her face, caressing her neck and ears as he wished he could. She smelled like no one he had ever been near before . . . except Dee Farris. He drew in a deep breath and slid a hand under her hair, drawing it out from within her collar, letting it fall like a root beer–colored stream over the blond fur.

His body tightened with the need to turn her into his arms, push his hands inside her coat, and hold her. She straightened her hair, slung the strap of a small purse over her shoulder, and stepped away.

He offered her his arm, and tucking her hand into the crook of his elbow, she picked up the basket of vegetables with the other. "These are for the doorman," she said as the bead curtain rattled behind them.

She smiled aloofly as she reached back through it and closed the glass doors. "Easier this time, isn't it?"

"Easier?" he echoed. She had no idea what she was talking about if she thought this was going to be an easy evening for him. She got to him in ways he hadn't been got to for a long time. What was it, simply an echo of the past? Or something a whole lot more important?

"No Mrs. Kimball to check you out with what you used to refer to as 'accusing eyes,'" she said.

He laughed, then ushered her into the elevator, which stood open and waiting. "That's one thing I never forgot. No matter how many times I came to pick you up, she regarded me as a potential rapist. Maybe she could read my mind," he said softly.

"You could never have been that," she said ruefully. "Not with me. I was very . . . willing." *But not now*, she didn't say, but he heard the words as clearly as if she'd shouted them.

"I wanted you from the first moment I saw you." *Even when I left you, I still wanted you. I simply knew I couldn't have you.*

She laughed. "No, you didn't. The first moment you saw me, you were too busy spitting out snow and curses to even notice that I was a woman."

"You weren't a woman, Dee. Not when I first met you."

"We've been over that several times," she said as the elevator moved slowly downward. "I was a woman who simply hadn't had a chance to prove it. You're not still doing the guilt thing about my virginity, are you?"

He shook his head. "No, of course not. But you were only a girl, Dee." He smiled to remind her of what he had once called her. "A kid."

He lowered his voice as he stroked a hand under her chin until it was lost in the fur surrounding her neck. "But you soon became a woman. Despite the vigilance of your bodyguard's rape watch."

She looked away quickly from the intensity in his eyes, and then the elevator came to a halt. Thank goodness. The doors eased open.

"Mrs. Kimball was my housekeeper."

He grinned. "Bodyguard."

Dee conceded with a nod. "All right, so my parents didn't trust me to look after myself adequately." Her parents had only agreed to her living off campus in a house with three other young women who rented rooms from her if she did it in a manner they considered safe: with a responsible adult in charge. They'd sent along Mrs. Kimball, who had been in their employ since Dee's early childhood.

"She meant well, and there was nothing personal in her attitude toward you," she said as her heels clicked across the marble floor. "She looked at every man as a potential rapist. My housemates' boyfriends were as paranoid about her as you were."

"A taxi, sir?" Jenkins said, after thanking Dee for the vegetables.

"Do you still see your housemates?" Matt asked as the doorman went out the double doors and down the broad stairs under the arched canopy to the street below.

"Not for a long time. Not since Mrs. Kimball's funeral, about ten years ago."

"I'm sorry," he said politely. "I hadn't heard of her death. I know you were fond of her."

"There was no reason for you to have heard," she said, "unless someone else told you. You and I—" She broke off, reminding herself again that it was far too late for recriminations.

Dee saw a certain tautness in his face as he glanced down at her. "Yes, we'd lost touch by then." She thought she saw memories of pain in his eyes, a residue of anger. Anger? Directed at her? But why? Because of who she was? Because of the family she came from?

"It was not by my choice that we . . . lost touch," she reminded him. A sudden whip of thirteen-year-old fury swept over her. "*I* returned to McGill. You did not."

He shrugged as if none of this mattered now. "It wasn't . . . possible."

"Neither was a phone call?"

"I wrote to you."

"Of course. Two paragraphs. It's been nice, but it's over. No explanation, no return address. No . . . hope."

"Dee, admit it. A clean break was better. Easier."

Maybe there were things that had to be said, after all. "Better? Easier? For whom, Matt?"

His brief glance held a kind of bleakness she'd seen

only rarely in his eyes. His voice was tight. "For you, I'd hoped."

"You were wrong."

He didn't comment on that. A muscle jumped spasmodically in his jaw.

Dee sighed silently. "Your family, Matt? How are they? When you left that summer, your father was ill. Did he . . . ?"

"He recovered," he said dismissively. He'd never said much about his family, apart from the basic facts. He'd been raised in Nova Scotia, his mother had died not long before Dee had met him, he had three brothers, all younger, and his father was—or had been—a Cape Breton coal miner.

"How are your brothers doing?"

At once he relaxed, and pride shone in his face. "Fine. Just fine, all three of them. Martin and Colin are married, both have kids, and Ron, he's the youngest, is engaged to a girl he met in dental school. They both graduated from Dalhousie last year and have set up practice together."

"Good for him. For them."

Dalhousie. The oldest, largest university in the Atlantic region. "Matt?"

"Yes?" He looked wary, as if he knew what was coming.

"Is that where you went? Dalhousie? Where you took your law degree?"

He concentrated on a brass plaque telling the building's age. "Yes."

"Why?" It was scarcely more than a whisper of sound, but it seemed to tear into the silence of the foyer like an echo, full of blame, full of the anguish she had experienced, as if it embodied all the questions she had asked of the wind and the skies and herself, but never of Matt until now.

He squared his shoulders and set his feet side by side with careful precision. "My father was ill, Dee. You knew that. He needed me. My brothers needed me. I was the oldest. It was my place to be there."

"I needed you too."

He smiled thinly. "Dee . . . You had everything you could have possibly needed. Nothing I could have given you would have been good enough. I had nothing. I was nothing. And when I got home again, away from you, I saw that more clearly than ever before. I saw . . . reality."

"And that reality was that *you* did not need *me*." She tried to smile. "It was my fault, wasn't it, for begging you to take me with you, and for offering you money?"

He looked away, stared at the doorman's uniformed back. A muscle jumped in his jaw.

Dee clenched her hands in her coat pockets.

Maybe Matt had been right after all. Once they'd completed the "remember so-and-so" routine, it could become a boring evening. Or at least a very strained one.

She stared at the wet black street, the reflected lights, hoping it wouldn't take too long for a taxi to cruise by. She wondered why she didn't simply say good night, turn, and go back upstairs before this aching silence grew any thicker. She was more used to spending her free evenings growing things than she was trying to think up small talk that would cover the memories of all the mistakes she'd made through youth and inexperience.

Mistakes. Lord, so many mistakes in her life. And agreeing to this date was yet another.

"Matt . . ."

His voice came in unison. "Dee . . ."

Their gazes locked as tightly as her fists were clenched. They both smiled tentatively. His smile looked so unwilling that a great knot of pain tightened inside her. She tried to speak again, but nothing came out.

"Ah, Dee." He placed his right hand on the back of her neck, sliding it under her hair again. Gently, he eased her toward him. She knew what he was going to do. She knew she could stop it before it even got started. She knew there were innumerable reasons not to let it happen, but the heavy, deep pounding inside her had to be relieved, the knot untied.

"I'm sorry I hurt you," he whispered, his breath warm against her cheek. He licked his lips, placed his left hand along her jaw, and tilted her head back. "I . . . had to leave when I did," he said. "And I had to leave you behind."

"I know." Oddly enough, she did know. Thirteen years earlier she'd understood, even through her pain, that his pain must have been as great. She knew he had loved her. She rested one hand on his chest, in the V at the front of his belted trench coat. "I'm sorry it all hurt you too." The blue and gray silk of his tie lay under her fingertips. His heart hammered so hard against her palm that she felt the vibration right into her bones.

"I need, very much," he whispered, "to kiss you, Dee."

"Yes." Her fingers tightened around his tie as she pulled him toward her. "I need that too."

It was a gentle kiss, one of remembrance, and possibly one of renewal. Softly, he tasted her. An underlying need threatened to take over, but he restrained it, held back. As she parted her lips for him, his fingers tightened momentarily on her nape; his other hand trembled for a second as he slid it along her jawline and under her ear. Once, he swept his tongue across hers. Once, he flexed his hand and arched her neck. Once, he made a sound like a poorly suppressed groan, and then it was over.

She drew in a tremulous breath, and it sighed out, sadly. The knot inside her had only grown tighter.

Matt pressed Dee to his chest and held her for a long, poignant moment, resting his cheek on her hair, breathing in the scent of her. Lifting his head, he tilted her head back and watched her lashes flutter open as he stroked her face. He slid his hand down her shoulder and arm, imagining, through the thickness of her coat, exactly what she felt like. Remembering. He laced his fingers with hers and lifted her hand, turning it over, placing his lips in the center of her palm.

She sighed softly again and withdrew her hand, stuffing it back into her pocket.

"Where are we dining?" she asked as Jenkins came back up the stairs. A taxi stood at the curb. She sounded completely detached, Matt thought.

"The Top of Vancouver," he said. He could disassociate himself too. "I decided to play the tourist thing to the hilt and take in the view. The concierge in my hotel says it's spectacular, as long as it's not foggy."

"I enjoy watching the scenes roll around," she said, "even when there's fog. That can add a note of mystery. The Top has been one of my favorites since I moved here."

"And when was that?" He handed the doorman a tip.

"Five years ago." She slid across the backseat to make room for him in the cab. "Just after my father passed away."

Her *father*? "Oh, Dee!" He knew how she'd idolized her father. Hell! He should have been there for her, to help her through it, to . . . He shook his head. "I'm sorry, kid. I had no idea. Was it sudden?" The ambassador would have been only in his early sixties.

She nodded, and stared out the window as the car started moving. She wanted to speak but couldn't. She swallowed hard, tightening her hands together. She'd thought the grieving all done. Why did having Matt beside her bring the pain back so sharply? Because losing Gavin had reminded her of losing Matt?

"Tell me about it, Dee," he said, freeing one of her hands from his tight clasp and holding it on the seat between them.

The knot inside her began to unravel, but she said nothing.

While they sipped drinks, waiting for their dinner, Dee's melancholy faded, and she pointed out different landmarks as the restaurant slowly revolved. Over smoked-salmon appetizers, served as the fairy lights in the trees of Gastown disappeared behind Matt, something he said elicited a chuckle. Then, with reminders of people they'd known, concerts they'd attended, and movies they'd shared, he soon had her laughing. It felt good. No one had ever made her laugh the way Matt could.

With their main courses before them, chicken breast stuffed with shrimp and scallops for her, rack of lamb for him, he told her a bit about Metcom. She told him about running Sheer Delight, about the renovations already in the works at her number-one store, her expansion into the premises previously occupied by a hair salon.

"It allows us to nearly double our retail space and will give Gail, my secretary, room to breathe between her desk and the wall. The contractors have just begun. It'll be expensive, making the leasehold improvements, but worth it in the long run. You saw how tiny the store is. Gail's office and mine are even smaller."

He nodded, and she thought she saw a frown cross his brow for an instant. But it must have been a passing worry, because his expression smoothed out almost at once. Under his interested questioning she went on talking enthusiastically about her boutiques.

When one waiter had cleared their plates and another brought coffee and liqueurs, and the "remember so-and-so" tradition had been observed, she was nowhere near being bored. Immersed in telling him about "Hometown Tourist," the column she wrote for a local weekly, Dee wanted only to spend the rest of the night talking with Matt.

"There are so many places around town that locals never think to visit," she said. "When I first came here, I was"—she shrugged, not really liking to admit it—"I guess lonely's the only word. And I had visited the area only briefly, stopping over to or from skiing in Whistler. All I'd seen were the usual tourist spots, so I started exploring, seeking out-of-the-way attractions. I soon found that I could take an excursion from my home every day for a year and still not find all the points of interest, both indoors and out.

"I've made more friends than I could have dreamed and discovered such intriguing places that I knew I had to share it. The column's been very well received."

"What are you featuring this week?" he asked, and

when she told him about the little out-of-the-way bakery that made the best pastries ever, he promised to go there the first time he had a few spare moments.

"What I'd really like to find," she said, leaning her chin on her hand, "is a place that sells real, honest-to-goodness Montreal smoked meat. That's one thing I can't seem to find here. There are lots of imitations, but none even approaching the real thing. Remember how good that was?"

For several minutes they shared other memories, then Dee said, "And what do you do with your spare time, Matt?"

He laughed. "Spare time? What's that?" Then, sobering, he went on, "I don't have much, but when I can, I ski, play handball, and . . ." He shrugged and added, diffidently, she thought, "I do some volunteer work for a consumer-advocacy group in Toronto."

She leaned forward, interested. "Class-action suits, that sort of thing?"

He nodded while concentrating on pouring milk into his coffee.

Dee smiled. "So you are out there defending the defenseless."

He glanced up. "A bit, I guess. But only a bit. I mostly interpret corporate jargon for consumer groups. Anybody could do that."

"Anybody could not! Why put yourself down, Matt? You're doing your part. You should be proud."

He shrugged again and changed the subject. Matt had always resisted talking about himself.

As the discussion swung into a heated one on current affairs, Dee sat forward in her chair, watching his eyes light up as he agreed with her, or his brows draw together as he told her she was crazy—which he did often and forcefully.

He'd never pulled his punches before, and he didn't now. She liked that about him. Among other things. He treated her with the same respect he would any other intelligent person active in business. If they didn't always agree on methods, they did agree that the bottom line was important, but so was satisfaction in a job well done.

Arguing with him was even more stimulating than getting along perfectly. For an instant she found herself remembering how well she and Gavin had gotten along, how smoothly they had worked together, but then Matt said something provocative, and she knew she couldn't waste any of this evening thinking of another man.

Matt filled up the world too well all by himself.

"It's the Asian influx that has Metcom interested in acquiring West Coast properties," he said. "Until recent years, we've kept most of our focus on eastern North American markets, but the pendulum of influence is swinging more and more to Vancouver, Seattle, San Francisco, as money pours around the Pacific Rim.

"And pour it does, not only investment capital, but the tourist dollars, too, or maybe I should say yen," Dee said.

"I have such a large percentage of Japanese customers that in tourist season I hire staff who speak the language. It pays off in increased sales. I also advertise over there, and in in-flight magazines with the various airlines. Did you see my ad in your hotel directory?"

He grinned and reached across the table to touch her hand. "I did—once I knew that my Delight owned Sheer Delight. Before that, I must confess, I hadn't paid much attention to the ads, though I did notice that many of them were in several languages."

My Delight? Her heart lurched. Then she reminded herself that not even when they were lovers had he called her that. He'd become a lot smoother over the years, a lot more sophisticated. He could say sweet things now, but because he could do it so easily, it likely meant much less. He'd honed his skills on other women.

"And they say it pays to advertise!" she complained. "You're living proof of the futility. Hotel guests are intended to *read* those ads. Did I waste my money?"

Matt laughed. "Now, maybe if I'd been in need of ladies' lingerie, I'd have read the ad when I first looked through the book."

Right. "If you weren't in need of it, what made you come into my store?"

He gave her a long, pensive look, as if trying to decide how to reply. "Maybe I've grown kinky in my old age?"

She returned the look with a reproachful one. "And maybe you haven't."

He grinned, refusing to be challenged. "Just remember, I came, I looked, but I didn't buy anything."

"I did notice that," she agreed. It hurt that he refused to tell her the truth. The older, more urbane, and smoother Matt hid as much as the younger one had, but whether it was from the same sense of defensiveness, she could only guess.

"I was extremely tempted by your very beautiful, very alluring wares, Ms. Farris," he said, "and I may well yet . . . partake." His smile, slow and sexy and half-hidden behind his lashes, suggested that he wasn't referring to the "wares" in her store.

She swallowed the excited little flutter that thrust up through her good sense again.

"And you came to the coast to buy, not lingerie but property," she said. "May I ask what property?"

He hesitated, and once more she detected a troubled expression in his eyes. "That's . . . uncertain," he said slowly. "We're looking at several possibilities."

Dee nodded. Of course. It didn't surprise her to learn that Matt's personal integrity remained intact. She smiled. "Forgive me. That was an unfair question. Of course you can't divulge details of your employer's business."

"There's nothing to forgive." Matt wished, suddenly, that he could tell her the truth. He could not, of course. Still, it felt almost like disloyalty, keeping Metcom's negotiations regarding the Westmarch Apartment Hotel secret from her, a tenant in the building. Yet his loyalty belonged to the company that paid his not inconsiderable salary. It also belonged to the founder of that company, Edwin James, who had taken Matt in right out of law school and helped him at every turn.

"It was a perfectly legitimate question," he went on, and found himself stroking her hand again. He wrapped his fingers around it. He couldn't stop touching her. It was a need that went even deeper than it had before.

"There are a couple of properties we have options on, and another two or three we're investigating. This is only the beginning of our expansion in the West," he continued. "The next decade could be crucial to Vancouver's— the entire Lower Mainland's—development. Companies who want in have to get in now, or it'll be too late." He shrugged as if to say it hardly merited discussion. "And Metcom wants in."

"So that means you'll be coming back here again?" Dizziness assailed Dee, a result of the almost unbearable mixture of emotions that washed through her. She could only hope Matt wasn't aware of her rising pulse rate. Oh, Lord, what was she doing? What was happening to her? It was all she could do to remind herself of the way he had hurt her once. Too large a part of her insisted that was then, this is now.

He nodded. "Yes. I'll be back here frequently." Then, as if he could read her as well now as he once had, he added softly, "It also means I intend to see you again, Dee."

She slid her hand out from under his and laid it on her lap with her other one. Both trembled.

"No, Matt." Her voice was soft but definite. Because, despite the sweetness of that kiss they'd shared earlier, that kiss they'd both agreed was utterly necessary, she intended to keep a tight rein on things.

Mostly on her own heart.

She knew how vulnerable it was.

"No," she said again, as much to herself as to him.

"Oh, yes, Dee," he said in firm contradiction.

As he said it, Matt knew he was committing himself to something he should not, at least until negotiations were finalized with Chang International, the present owners of the Westmarch. It could certainly be seen as conflict of interests, and if a leak occurred . . .

But he couldn't help himself. He'd known from the moment he'd seen Dee that things were likely to escalate rapidly between them. He was vitally aware that she knew it, too, and was afraid. The tremor in her voice was proof of that. He could even understand her fear.

"Matt—" she said, then broke off, looking down.

Oh, yes, he said again silently as he studied the faintly blue tinge of her lowered lids, the flush of color in her cheeks, the moist thrust of her full lower lip. One way or another, things were going to happen between them. Either the old feelings—old feelings he was barely able to contain just sitting across from her—would flare up briefly like a star becoming a nova, then die back down, or they'd ignite and maintain a steady, relentless heat that would burn him to his core.

He didn't know which he wanted more. Or dreaded the most.

"My life is very . . . full, just now," she said with a cool, polite smile that completely belied the flags of color in her cheeks. "I don't have much time for being sociable—as my mother would regretfully attest. Although I do spend most weekends with her in Victoria."

She paused. "I also go on periodic buying trips to various parts of the world. London, Rome, Paris, Madrid. And Asia."

Toronto, too, and frequently, she didn't say.

"It was pure luck that you found me where you did today."

It was also pure luck, though at this point she couldn't have said good or bad, that they had never stumbled over each other in Toronto. "Often," she continued, "I'm not there for days at a time."

She smiled again, much the way he'd seen Queen Elizabeth smile on television. "Next week I'm going to Paris."

He captured her gaze and said roughly, "It won't work. You can't get rid of me, Dee, not that easily."

Dammit, he knew he was getting too intense too fast. With effort he smoothed out his tones. "I'll be in and out of town regularly over the next few months." He smiled.

"And I won't ask you to be . . . sociable. I'll simply ask you to be with me."

Dee shivered deep inside. She and Matt together, not being "sociable," meant, simply, she and Matt . . . together. Alone.

She shook her head and changed the subject.

With a shrug he let the matter drop. Dee was glad. It was time to go home.

THREE

"Let's walk," she said as they emerged from the restaurant to find the rain had stopped and the clouds had blown away. It would be better than the close confines of a taxi.

Matt glanced down at her high heels. "Can you walk in those shoes?"

"No problem. They're very comfortable."

He took her hand and said doubtfully, "Well, if you're sure. But if you get tired, tell me, and I'll get a taxi."

Dee laughed at him as she squeezed his fingers. "You worry too much." It was pleasant, being worried about. "Come on. It's not far, and it's a nice night." It was cool and crisp, with a hint of the frost that might come before morning. A clear night was rare for that time of year. Snowcapped, the North Shore mountains glowed high above the city under a crescent moon.

"Pretty, isn't it?" Matt asked, following the direction of her gaze.

"Yes. I never tire of looking at the hills. They're almost as captivating as the ocean." From her penthouse windows and terraces she had an excellent range of view, one of the reasons she'd chosen to live there. Her advisers kept prodding her to buy a place of her own, rather than pour money into a home in which she was building no equity. But her place suited her, and the building had been in the same hands for nearly twenty years. There was no reason to think that was likely to change any time soon.

"It's the first time I've seen the mountains since I've been here this trip," Matt said. "They've been buried in clouds for the past few days."

"Don't complain," she said. "This time of year, often when it's raining down here, it's snowing up there. The people of this city are very proud of being able to sail, play golf, and ski all on the same day and all within twenty minutes of downtown."

They turned their backs on the mountains and walked south across the West End peninsula toward English Bay. "Do you spend any of that spare time of yours up on the slopes?"

"No," Dee said. "I haven't been skiing since I opened the first store."

"What? And you live within twenty minutes of three ski hills?"

"I wish I could, but as I said, my spare time is scarce. You?"

"Not recently. I was hoping I might manage a run or two this trip," he said, "though I didn't realize until this past weekend that I should have brought my ski gear. I hadn't anticipated the West Coast businessman's propensity for taking weekends off. Our current negotiations aren't likely to be completed before the middle of next week, so I'll be in town over the coming weekend. Maybe . . ." He let the thought trail off.

Dee glanced over her shoulder at the gleaming peaks. "It's too bad it's so early in the season. They may look good from down here, but the base won't likely be deep enough up there until around Christmas, so they aren't open. Whistler and Blackcomb both are, though. They're only a ninety-minute drive away," she added. "I'm certain you could rent everything you need up there."

She hesitated for a moment. "And I have a little place on the outskirts of Whistler Village that you'd be welcome to use. I don't think I've promised it to anyone else for the next couple of weeks."

He stopped. "You have a place in Whistler, and you haven't been skiing in five years?"

Dee shrugged. "As I said, I've been busy. I suppose I should sell it, but my advisers say it's a good investment, and I do have friends who enjoy using it. My mother takes visitors up there periodically, too, but . . ." She took off one of her gloves, then put it back on, smoothing the fingers. "But . . ."

"But you don't. Why, Dee?"

She avoided his gaze. "I . . . just haven't wanted to. Come one, let's walk on. It's getting colder."

Matt didn't speak for nearly two blocks. Then, he said, "What is it about your place in Whistler that makes you sad, Dee?"

She gave him a startled look. "It doesn't!" The denial was as automatic as it was false.

He held her gaze. "It does."

She compressed her mouth. Matt had always been able to pick up on her moods.

"Why won't you talk about it?"

"Because . . . you're right. It does make me sad. I guess I've been foolish to keep it, under the circumstances, but maybe I've hoped that time would ease my feelings. It's all tied up in my mind with one of the most unhappy periods in my life.

"I bought the place a couple of weeks before my father died. It was supposed to be a surprise for my husband-to-be."

Husband! The word hit Matt's chest like a hammer blow, and he nearly staggered before he caught himself. Dammit, the notion shouldn't be so foreign. He'd realized that she must have had relationships with other men. Yet he had to fight down the image of some other man's hands on her, molding her shape, making love to her. He had to clench his fists against the need to punch someone. Some man who had hurt Dee, put that sad, despairing look into her eyes.

"What happened?" he asked tautly.

"When my father passed away, naturally, we postponed the wedding. Then . . . things changed between us, and we . . . never resumed our plans."

Matt was sure there was a lot more to it than that. Things changed. What things? He wanted to know the details almost as badly as he dreaded hearing them, but before he could ask, she said, "Like most events that appear as disasters at the time, that one had a happy outcome, though."

"What was that?"

She laughed, and his heart lightened. She might have been hurt by an experience five years earlier, but not irrevocably. "That broken engagement propelled me into opening my first store."

"Why?"

"Gavin, my former fiancé, was the publisher of the news magazine I worked for in San Francisco," she said. "It would have been awkward continuing there, even staying in the same city, so I needed something else, somewhere else. My parents had moved to Victoria when Dad retired from the diplomatic service, and after he died, I wanted to be near my mother. I came north.

"Vancouver Island doesn't have the population base of the Lower Mainland, so from a marketing viewpoint it made better sense for me to set up operations here in Vancouver."

"Running a boutique."

"Yes. Almost at once I found I really enjoyed it. It seems I was more than ready for something different."

"I guess it was different," he said. "From journalism to retail? Quite a change. Buy why lingerie?" Books, given her partialities, or magazines, he could have understood.

She smiled up at him, and he was relieved to see not a hint of her former sadness in her eyes. "When I—by the time Gavin and I decided it wasn't going to work out between us, I'd already had four quite large wedding showers, and as luck would have it, three of them were lingerie showers."

His mouth gaped for a second. "Your trousseau became the first stock for your store?"

Her gay laughter rang out. He loved hearing it, loved seeing her eyes bright with amusement. *"Matt!* Of course not. That would have been in extremely bad taste.

"Oh, my goodness!" She put a hand over her mouth for a second and flicked a laughing glance at him. "I wonder how many of my friends—and my mother's— suspect I did just that? After all, I must have received ten years' worth of undergarments and nightwear. It would have been enough to stock a small boutique. Oh, I do hope none of them believe that of me. I offered the gifts back to them, of course, but no one accepted."

Matt had to laugh at the idea of those ever-so-polite ladies wondering secretly if Dee had done something so tacky as sell off her trousseau. "So how did getting those things induce you to open a boutique?"

"I started thinking, if my friends bought that many garments as shower gifts for one bride-to-be, there had to be a large market out there. And I wanted something totally absorbing to do. I thought it would take my mind off my troubles, to focus on other things."

His mind was on those very same other "things" Dee had been focusing on for the past five years. Pretty things. On Dee's pretty body.

He gave her a long, slow look. "So what did you do with all those dainties you received as shower gifts?" he asked. "Put them away for the next honeymoon you might find yourself planning?"

"Of course not. I . . . used them. Use them. Wear them." She paused. "A woman likes to be beautifully dressed from the skin out every day, not only on her honeymoon."

Matt's mind filled with images. Dee's bedroom closets, her chests of drawers, overflowing with sheer, delightful garments. He could see them: pastels, blacks, whites, bright jewel tones. With lace, with feathers, with ribbons and bows. Enough to stock a store. A ten-year supply. And only five years had passed. He could see them spread across her bed, see them draped over the shower rail. See them on her. He swallowed hard. He could see them coming off her, very, very slowly.

"Every day?" he asked. His voice was hoarse. "To-day?"

She smiled as they approached the steps leading up to her building's entrance. "Matt, it's been a lovely evening. Thank you so very much." She held out her hand. "Good night."

Matt laughed. "Good *night*?" He snatched the hand she offered, and held it tightly as she would have escaped. "Not yet, kid. It's nowhere near time to say good night."

The evening, and the discussion, were not over yet. Not as far as Matt was concerned. Pulling her hand into the crook of his arm, he held her at his side, walking on as the ever-vigilant and protective doorman left his post and descended two stairs.

Matt steered Dee to the curb. "About Whistler," he said, as a break in traffic permitted them to cross the road to the broad walkway at the top of the beach. "If I accept your offer of the loan of your place, would you go with me?"

"No!" Dee snatched her elbow away. Her breath caught in her throat. She bit her lip and steadied herself, linking her hands together. "Thank you, but no," she said more evenly. "I . . . won't have the time. I'm not the kind of businessperson who takes many weekends off," she fibbed, forgetting she'd told him she spent most weekends with her mother.

Matt turned her face up to his and looked at her long and searchingly in the glow of a streetlight. "Coward."

She bridled and twisted away. "That's not fair! I *am* busy."

"Busy, sure. And scared."

She frowned. "All right. I already told you. I don't like the place, Matt. It brings back too many bad memories. I was there when the news came that my father was gone. If you want to call me a coward for avoiding it after that, then fine. But I think people have a right to protect themselves against hurt. Especially unnecessary hurt."

"I'm sorry the place has bad memories for you," he said evenly, but his gaze was shrewdly penetrating. "However, I know that's not your reason for refusing, Dee. Whether you're willing to admit it to yourself or not, you're afraid to go there with *me*. I recognize a panicky no when I hear one."

Dee gritted her teeth. Matt had never let her get away with being less than truthful, especially to herself. He tapped her chin with one finger. "Your refusal to go has less to do with the past than it does the present. Right, Dee?"

Dee met his gaze. It was pointless to try to lie to him. "Fine," she said again haughtily. "I admit it. But I have a right to protect myself against that kind of . . . trauma, too, don't I?"

"Why would a weekend with me be traumatic?"

She met his gaze squarely. "Perhaps it wouldn't be.

Maybe it's the time after it that concerns me. The time when you go back to your real life and your . . ."

His gaze narrowed sharply. "My what?"

She knew she might not like the answer, but she had to ask the question. "You came into my shop to make a purchase, Matt. I can only assume you had a woman in mind as a recipient for whatever you bought. She must be important to you. And you to her. Why, with her in your life, are you coming on to me?"

Matt puffed out a frustrated breath. Dammit, he couldn't tell her why he'd gone into her store initially. Both Metcom and the present owners of the building wanted their negotiations kept completely confidential, for valid reasons.

"Dee," he said, "I'm not 'coming on to' you. I'm—" He broke off with a disgusted grimace. Hell, of course he was coming on to her. Dee was no fool. And she had a right to an answer.

"All right," he said, "I did come into your store with a purpose, but it was not to buy anything for anyone. There is no woman in my life now."

"This purpose?" she asked. "I suppose it's not one you'd care to share with me?"

He tried to keep his tone casual. "My purpose for coming into your store was as I said, the name intrigued me, and that teddy in the window told me there'd be other things worth . . . admiring. I went into the building, though, because I like old buildings."

Dee remembered that from the past. Luckily, she liked old buildings, too, or she'd have grown tired of being dragged through Montreal's most ancient ones. All right. She supposed it was as much explanation as she was going to get from him, and while it didn't entirely satisfy her, she had to let it go at that.

"And," Matt continued his argument, "since there's no man in your life, what's to stop either of us spending a weekend skiing with an old friend?"

She tugged off one glove, then the other, and stood slapping the soft kid leather against her wrist. The same argument, almost word for word, had persuaded her to have dinner with him. Did he think it would work for a weekend too? Obviously, he did.

Then, flicking a glance up at him, she asked, "Is that what we're talking about, Matt?"

He closed his eyes for a moment. Of course it wasn't. Not entirely. But it could be. If it had to be.

"If that's all you want to talk about, then yes. If you went with me, you wouldn't have to concern yourself with . . . I assume your chalet has more than one bedroom?" Most of the ski-hill A-frames he'd seen did. If not, there'd surely be a sofa bed. She'd said she loaned the place to friends. "You'd have nothing to fear in that way. All I'm asking for is a weekend on the slopes, not one in the sack."

She flung her head back, offended. "That was crude."

His chuckle held little humor. "Remember? I'm not

one of your sugar-coated gentlemen. I am crude at times. It's my heritage. But we've both known for a long time that your heritage and mine aren't comparable. I happen to prefer mine. It's less . . . artificial."

"Matt . . ." There was a distinct warning in her tone. "I won't listen to your reverse snobbery. There's no need for it, and it doesn't become you."

He sighed again. "Sorry. Still, I'd like to think that you know me better than to fear I'd ever force you, or even try to seduce you."

He slipped his fingers through hers. "When you come to me, you'll do it the same way you always did: openly, eagerly, wanting me as much as I want you . . . before we so much as kiss."

"Matt . . . I won't be—"

She broke off with a soft intake of breath as he ran the tips of his fingers down her face and under her chin. His husky, whispered "Remember?" sent shivers down her back and legs.

Oh, how well she remembered. Simply a glance across a crowded room could send them both heading for the door, to slip away from their friends and find privacy, somewhere, anywhere, while they tried to slake their mutual need.

She slid her hand up his arm to his wrist and wrapped her fingers around it, pulling his hand from her face. Automatically, she laced her fingers with his, liking the feel of his warm, dry palm against hers. "Matt . . . don't make me remember those things."

His look challenged her to try to forget. All he said, though, was, "About this weekend . . . think about it, Dee. Think about the fun we used to have together, skiing. We could recapture all of that."

Somehow, Dee heard a silent *And more* follow his words. But the words had arisen only in her mind and heart, like new grass in the spring.

Again she shook her head. "I explained. I spend most weekends with my mother."

"This coming weekend, specifically?"

She frowned, hesitated, then realized he had no way of knowing if she was telling the truth or not. "Yes."

He laughed lazily. "You're lying, Dee."

She glared indignantly. "Matt . . ."

"You blush when you lie. Did you think I'd have forgotten that little thing?"

"I'm not blushing. My cheeks are red from the cold."

He shook his head. "You blush, and a muscle right there"—he touched the left side of her jaw, under her ear—"jumps like crazy."

"Oh." She slid her fingers from his and stuffed her hand into her pocket.

He said nothing more about it, though, but pulled her hand from her pocket and held it in his as they walked back to her building and up the steps.

"You don't need to come up with me," she said as they entered the foyer.

"I told you. I pick my date up, and I see her right to her door."

She inserted her key in the wall at the side of the private elevator. "This is my door."

He grinned. "I see my date right onto her front porch," he said, and stepped into the elevator with her. As the doors closed, he parted her hair at her nape and kissed the back of her neck. She closed her eyes and gripped her purse as a strong shudder swept through her.

"Please!" It was a taut sound. "You said you wouldn't seduce me."

He turned her to face him, his hands strong and hard on her upper arms. "I'm not seducing you. I'm merely making it clear what I'm feeling. If there's any seduction going on, it's in your own mind."

She bit her lip. He was right. What was it someone had said? That the most sensitive erogenous zone was located between the ears? All evening she'd been remembering the way it had been, thinking, consciously and subconsciously, about the way it could be again, with her and Matt. His every touch, the sound of his voice, the laughter in his eyes, had reinforced her yearning.

His eyes, dark now, held her gaze, controlled it, compelling her to think about what he was saying. As well as what he was not. It was what he was not telling her that bothered her.

"Ah . . . don't," she whispered, trying to stop her hand from curving around his jaw.

He put his hand over hers, holding it to him. "It won't work, Dee, telling me 'Don't.' Eventually, I'm going to. And you're going to."

She drew in a tremulous breath and stepped back from him. With a toss of her head she flicked her hair back into place. She managed a creditable laugh and a suitably amused smile, as if he presented no danger at all. "I'm going to what?"

He grinned at her haughty accents, and bowed sweepingly as the elevator came to a halt, the doors whispering open. "Your floor, I believe, duchess."

As he ushered her onto her "front porch," he smiled again, that bold, confident look that had once captivated her blazing from his eyes. The bad-boy look. She didn't know why he had it. He'd never really been one. Maybe it was knowing that he had the potential to be bad that had excited her so much. That still did.

He cupped his hand around her nape and tipped her head back. "You're going to love every last, long minute of it," he said, his voice barely above a whisper. "Just the way you used to."

Despite the surge of heat his words provoked, she gave him what she hoped was a poised smile that indicated her firm lack of intention to succumb to a swift seduction. Or to a slow one. Even if it was all in her own mind.

Inside, though, she was eighteen again, eighteen and

madly in love for the first time in her life, aching for the kind of swift seduction she'd acceded to so willingly then. She wished she had something solid to hang on to, but the only thing available was Matt Fiedler, and simply looking at him made the ground shift under her feet.

It was long past time to say good night.

On a shaken whisper she said it, and added, "Thank you, Matt. It was a pleasant evening." To her amazement, even her relief, he simply brushed his mouth across hers, smiled, and backed into the elevator until their fingers finally slid apart. He pushed the button to descend to street level and watched her watching him as the doors slid shut between them.

Her blue eyes haunted him during the taxi ride back to his hotel. They hadn't been bright blue as she'd said good night that last time, but a dark, brooding navy shade, filled with shadows and moods.

It was a pleasant evening. Thank you. The duchess after a hot date.

Matt had to smile as he lay on his bed, remembering every detail of her, every shade and variation of expression, every second of his evening with Dee. He wished he could sleep, but his head was too full of disquieting thoughts.

Dee. So many changes in her life. Her father gone, her mother living in Victoria, undoubtedly in regal splendor he could never hope to attain. Nor want if he could have. It was splendor that Dee, as an only child, would inherit one day.

He thought of her penthouse, her thriving boutiques. Obviously, she had already inherited a great deal with her father's death.

Her father . . . He jammed two pillows together and leaned against the headboard, thinking about the large, aristocratic man who had come closer than any other person to instilling fear in him. If not that, then awe, certainly. Her father, Lincoln Farris, had been ambassador to the Court of St. James when Matt had met him.

As if that hadn't been enough for a green young man to contend with, there was her mother. Whew! British aristocracy from a family probably a thousand years old. Lady Helen. Daughter of an earl, no less.

At twenty-two, twenty-three, he hadn't been able to deal with all of that.

When he'd met Dee, she'd been just another little freshman. He'd been a senior, a man on top of things, a man with places to go, goals to meet. He likely wouldn't have noticed her, except she'd run her toboggan right over the tips of his skis and sent him headfirst into the thick branches of a pine tree. She'd frantically dug him free, and he'd spit out enough snow to berate her for having that damned toboggan on a ski run.

She'd halted his diatribe by holding up a hand that shouldn't have, but did, manage to look imperious though it was encased in a fuzzy red mitten. In her cool, meticulous accents she'd said, "Sir. Having spent my formative years in warmer climates, I am not fortunate enough to know how to ski. And snow is snow. Telling me that I can't use a toboggan on it is as illogical as saying that only Chevrolets can use the highways."

He'd flung back his head and roared with laughter, whereupon she'd slipped one foot between his cumbersome ski boots and unceremoniously shoved him back into the drifted-over pine boughs. By the time he'd fought his way out and stamped his boots back into his bindings, she was gone.

He'd eventually found her at the bottom, recognizing her dumb hat that looked like a bright red knitted head of hair with two long braids that flapped around her shoulders. He'd been too stupid then to recognize her haughty, aristocratic behavior as genuine, her birthright. It had, though, intrigued him. She had totally enchanted him.

And he'd taken it upon himself to teach her how to ski. And how to cook. And how to make love. At the first two, she'd been a slow and indifferent learner.

But that was all before he'd met her parents. He'd fallen in love with her before he knew that the son and grandson of coal miners had no business—and no future—with the granddaughter of a nobleman. Even now, he could recall the sense of despair he'd lived with in the weeks between March, when he'd met her parents, and the end of May, when he'd left McGill University with the unwilling promise that he'd return to Dee.

It was a promise he'd failed to keep. Long ago he'd

realized that even as he made it, it was empty of everything except bravado.

No matter how hard he tried to convince himself that he was as good as anyone else, he couldn't quite believe it. Over and over he told himself that such things as family and position and financial circumstances didn't matter, not to him, not to her. This was the twentieth century, not the seventeenth. He'd been raised in a classless society, lived in one. Democracy dictated that a man be known by what he'd accomplished, not by who his forefathers had been.

Dee had told him the same thing. But he'd known deep down that they were both wrong.

He'd left McGill when his father needed him at home, knowing he would never see Dee again. He'd felt like a coward for leaving her, for being afraid to compete for her against the immense weight of her family's wealth and traditions. But he'd have felt like a failure if he'd had to see her suffer as his mother had, struggle to cope with the grinding poverty of a Nova Scotia coal town. Eventually, he'd graduated in the top five of his class, and by the time he'd passed the bar, he'd successfully put the memories of his first real love out of his mind.

Except for the odd little lapse.

Was that the category to file tonight under?

Dee left her private elevator the next morning on the lobby level and nodded good morning to the doorman.

She crossed the marble floor, feeling as if she'd managed to escape the brunt of a dangerous storm. It had taken all her strength not to go down one more level to the parking garage, get into her car, drive the short distance to Matt's hotel, and ask the desk clerk to call his room. Just to see if he was in.

It was only because she'd wakened thinking of him maybe having breakfast all alone, she reasoned. Only because she remembered how he liked company when he ate. It would have cost her nothing to show him where she bought her favorite coffee and croissants. After all, he was a stranger in town. Or did he still stow down a huge breakfast of as many calories, as much cholesterol, as was sensible to eat in an entire day?

She thought of the breadth of his shoulders, the lean length of his legs, the powerful muscles she'd felt in his chest. He ate well, but sensibly. And he'd told her that he kept active playing handball.

She had to smile, thinking of the breakfasts they had shared, often in bed. Instant chocolate pudding and soda crackers, great chunks of Mennonite sausage washed down with flat beer. Whatever happened to be available in his bachelor apartment. Even cold pizza. The remains of Chinese takeout. And then, invariably, they'd been . . . active. Together. Not playing handball.

Was he sitting over his coffee, thinking about her?

Oh, stop it, she told herself. The man has been at work, in meetings, for hours already. He operated from a mind-set three time zones earlier than this one. If he'd had breakfast at all, it would have been with his colleagues, in one of the restaurants of his hotel, and they'd probably discussed dry, boring property deals as they ate.

When they weren't grousing about the laid-back, lazy West Coast people, who were never in as much hurry as those from the East.

She entered the store, startling Elise, the manager.

"My goodness! What are you doing in here today? I thought you were going to the Park Royal branch."

"I changed my mind," Dee said, feeling vaguely embarrassed, as if Elise might guess at any minute why she was there. Matt knew the location of this store, but not that of the others. "There were a couple of things I wanted to . . . take care of here this morning. I'll be in my office if . . . if anyone asks for me."

She strode past her equally startled secretary with scarcely a good morning, and shut the door of her office with more force than was absolutely necessary.

She'd spend enough time in there to justify her having shown up, then she'd leave. Matt was not going to come looking for her. And he was not thinking about her. So she wouldn't think about him. She dragged several folders from a filing cabinet, opened one of them on her desk, and stared at its contents, tapping the end of a pen against her teeth.

FOUR

With difficulty Matt tried again to force his mind to focus on the subject under discussion, which was his firm's proposed purchase of the Westmarch Apartment Hotel as part of a much larger parcel. He failed as the voices of the eight people sharing the boardroom with him droned on, each one making his or her report.

Until Monday morning, Matt had been of two minds what his recommendation would be about buying the Westmarch. As point man, he'd been in the city several days longer than his colleagues and boss. His walks throughout the six-block area east of the building had been encouraging. The area was run-down, but if they could get in on a promised government-funded urban-renewal program, meant to push back the creeping edges of downtown decay, they'd be in clover. Still, the West-march wasn't essential to the project and could in no way be categorized with the other properties offered by Chang International.

As a piece of prime waterfront, the land it stood on was worth more than the rest of the package put together.

He'd thought he was leaning more toward the positive, and then he'd discovered the boutique, and Dee Farris. It shouldn't have changed his way of thinking.

However, it had.

Now he could see more and stronger reasons for not buying the building. The land value being so much higher than that of the building meant that if Metcom bought it, he, along with Karl, the architect, who now sat across the table from him, would have a serious battle on their hands to save the Westmarch. And along with it, Dee's home, her boutique, and the leasehold improvements she'd already initiated. Would Edwin James, CEO of Metcom, take Matt and Karl's advice and keep the Westmarch intact, or would he insist on gutting it? If the latter happened, all Dee's improvements would be money down the drain. Her money. Her drain.

He frowned, wishing that Chang International had found some reason not to let her go ahead, though the company didn't want it publically known that their property was on the block. He tried to tell himself that Dee had more money than most boutique owners, that the loss wouldn't hurt her as much as it would the others who lived there or had their businesses on the main floor, but that wasn't the point, and he knew it. It was Dee he was most concerned for.

He sighed, also wishing that he could forget that Dee was no more than a five-minute taxi ride away.

He could visualize what it would be like, his walking into her store unexpectedly for a second time. Her big bright eyes would light up at the sight of him the way they had the day before. She'd pull in a long breath that lifted her round breasts high, and she'd smile. Her pink lips would part, and she'd say . . .

"Matt? Matt!"

Somebody poked him in the ribs. It was Marcia Longstreet, the company's chief financial officer.

He glanced up quickly from the page he'd been pretending to study. "What?"

Marcia gestured toward their boss.

Edwin stared at him curiously. "Yes, sir?" Matt said. "Sorry. I was . . . concentrating on something else."

"So I could see. Your opinion, please."

"I must confess, Edwin, it's not fully formed. I need more time to go over some details with the zoning-variance committee—who, by the way, would like you in on that meeting—and to talk terms of takeover with the attorneys from the other side. However, neither group will be available until tomorrow afternoon."

Then, feeling vaguely dishonorable, he mentioned his visits to the Westmarch, both alone and with Karl. He did not mention that he was personally acquainted with one of the tenants. "It's my recommendation that if we proceed with the purchase of Chang's full package, we either incorporate the Westmarch as it stands into our overall design proposal or accept the smaller package."

"I see." Edwin gave him a penetrating stare. "I don't suppose your recommendation would have anything to do with the building's being an old one?"

"It is an old building, Edwin," he agreed levelly. "But Karl and I both feel that it's sound. It's also worth preserving. Intact," he added pointedly. In other words no gutting simply to redo it in a style not befitting its period.

Karl concurred with a nod. "Of course, we'll need to check it out more thoroughly than we've done. And the city inspectors will have reports on its condition, its upgrading through the years."

"We'd bring in our own people as well, to look at it with Karl," Matt said. "The Westmarch could well become the keystone of the whole development. As a historical building, its design and structure could be used as a theme for the entire development. Right, Karl?"

Before Karl could reply, Edwin said dryly, "I detect a note of enthusiasm creeping into the discussion. It always happens, doesn't it, Matt, when you're trying to save some relic from the sweeping hand of progress? I'm glad you work for me, son, and not for the local Heritage Building Society." Was there a hint of warning in Edwin's tone? It wouldn't have been the first building over which he and Matt had gone head-to-head. But Edwin had not yet seen the Westmarch. Matt wished he could show his boss Dee's solarium.

"To my knowledge," Matt said, "the local heritage people haven't put it on their list."

"Good. And let's see that we keep it that way, hm?"

Another subtle warning. Leaks as to the Westmarch's inclusion in this purchase would not be looked upon favorably.

It came as a relief when, an hour later, Edwin rapped the edges of a document on the table, then shoved back his chair saying, "All right. That will be it for today, people. As Matt said, there's little we can do until he and I meet again with city hall. But we all have plenty of material to consider. We'll gather back here tomorrow morning at nine sharp, to discuss the financial statements. Feel free to take the rest of the day off, just so long as you go over Marcia's report. Marcy, will you be available for questions?"

She nodded, then, as Edwin marched out, rolled her eyes heavenward and muttered to Matt, "'Feel free to take the day off. . . .' Sure. Just be available for questions." She sighed. "Lunch, Matt? Phil?"

Matt shook his head. "Sorry. I have . . . something to do."

Several minutes later Matt leapt out of his cab in front of Dee's building.

And then he stopped. She had three stores. She'd been in this one the previous day. That was no guarantee she'd be in it now. He was wasting his time. Even if there was a chance of her being there, he was probably wasting his time. . . .

At 12:35 Dee knew she had wasted much more time than she should have. Moments later, with her jacket slung over her shoulder by one finger, she waved to the store's manager and left. The doorman saw her coming and swung the door wide for her, saluting as she went past him at a half-run. She was more than a little annoyed with herself, hanging around like a lovesick teenager, afraid to go ten paces from the telephone lest the boy of her dreams call and find her out.

She grimaced as she trotted down the stairs under the building's entrance canopy. When she'd actually been a lovesick teenager, it had been over the same man. When would she learn?

Matt came to a halt as he saw Dee step out from under the canopy into the sunshine. She was wearing a slim black skirt, a light gray sweater with pink swirls on one shoulder, and carrying her jacket. She blinked, glanced his way, and stood there, meeting his gaze from ten feet away.

He took another step forward. She did the same. A glad smile trembled on her lips.

"Lunch?" he asked, his voice rough.

Her eyes shone as she moved toward him, coming to a halt only half a pace away. "Yes," she said. "Lunch."

He draped an arm over her shoulder. "Where?"

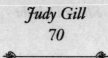
"I spent too much time thinking about you this morning," Matt said. They walked, hand in hand, along the seawall in Stanley Park, munching hot dogs. "My boss wasn't pleased with me. If having you on my mind costs me my job, will you be content with cheap dates like this all the time?"

Dee refused to dwell on the thought of more dates, cheap or not. She'd take the day, the moment, and enjoy.

"My downtown manager wasn't pleased with me either," she said. "I think she was afraid I was checking up on her when I showed up there this morning instead of going to one of the other stores, as I'd planned."

He lobbed his hot-dog wrapper into a garbage can. "What happened to your plans?" he asked slyly, and watched a flare of color spread over her cheekbones, color that she couldn't claim was caused by cold on this unexpectedly mild and sunny Tuesday afternoon.

He didn't insist on an answer but bent and picked a bronze chrysanthemum, tucking it into the buttonhole of her black suede blazer. She smiled. "You could go to jail for that, I think."

"No problem," he said. "I have a law degree, remember? I could talk my way out of it."

She laughed. "You, my friend, could do that before you were even close to a law degree."

He swung her hand to behind her back and pulled her against him. "And am I your friend really, Dee?"

She met his gaze, a wistful smile hovering on her lips, in her eyes. "Do you want to be?"

He nodded. "More than anything," he said, then grinned as he told the truth. "Well, more than almost anything."

"Oh, Matt . . . you—" She broke off and, for a moment, buried her face against the front of his coat.

"What?" he asked, a wave of the utmost tenderness roughening his voice as he held her close. "What were you going to say, Dee?"

"Nothing." She pushed herself away from him, and they walked on.

"Will you have dinner with me again tonight?" he asked, swinging their hands between them.

Dee shook her head. "I'm sorry. I have to write two columns this evening. They're due on my editor's desk tomorrow afternoon. Ordinarily, it would only be one, but because of that darned Paris trip, I have to get ahead of the game."

Paris. He stared at her. She was so casual about it. It was little more to her than a minor annoyance that meant she had to write an extra column. He'd traveled widely in his work, but he still experienced a secret thrill whenever he boarded an aircraft bound for a foreign country, a silent, *Well, Mom, whaddaya think of me now?*

"What places will you be writing about tonight?" he asked quickly. "They'll be for this coming Friday and the next?" He wondered if he could subscribe to her weekly, have the paper sent to his Toronto address for the time when he wasn't on the coast. Then he could phone Dee to comment, or question, or . . . He'd have an excuse to keep in touch. An excuse? Would he need one?

She nodded. "One of them's all but finished, so I really shouldn't complain. I found a real little gem of a place that delights me every time I go there. So that column will all but write itself. It's the other one that's giving me pain."

"Tell me about it," he said.

Evading his hand as he'd have taken hers again, she said, "It's a little park tucked in behind city hall, and as far as I can make out, about the only ones who use it are civic employees who have to go outside for a cigarette now that all city buildings are smoke-free. But there is a special feel to it that struck me the first time I wandered into it and continues to intrigue me. I've been trying to write about it for months, and tonight I absolutely must get it done. If I had anything else, I'd use it, but I don't."

"What's so hard about it?"

She frowned unhappily. "I don't know. For some reason every time I try to write it up, it's clear in my mind, but the message doesn't come through. And it's a pretty place, especially in the spring when the rhododendrons are in bloom, but even now, it has its charm."

So did she, and he still wanted to have dinner with her again. They had so much time to make up for. "Okay," he said, "so you have to stay home tonight and write your articles. What about tomorrow?"

"I'm sorry, Matt. No." She offered no explanation.

He wasn't about to give up. "Thursday?"

"Thursday's my night at the rape-crisis center. I man a phone line."

He gave her a long, scowling stare. Talk became general, a discussion of the sights they passed. Still, Dee didn't get the impression Matt had given up. She wasn't sure how she felt about that. She'd wanted to be with him, had enjoyed their time in the park, but there were so many unanswered questions in her mind, she didn't know if she should risk seeing him again.

Still, would those questions ever be answered if she didn't ask them? It was so hard to do, though. It went against all her training, all the well-bred reserve of generations behind her, to question another person. If a friend chose not to divulge details of his life, one must respect his privacy.

But did that dictate extend to someone who was more than just a friend? And was that what Matt wanted? More than friendship?

"May I offer you a lift back to your hotel?" she asked politely when they arrived back at her building. "I'm on my way to West Van, so it's no trouble. I'll just get the car out.

He shook his head. "No, thanks. I have the afternoon

off. I'll walk awhile. Who knows? Someday, I might want your job."

"What? Selling ladies' undies?"

Matt laughed and drew a thumb along her jawline. "I should be so lucky! No. I mean, seeking strange new places and boldly telling an appreciative public about them."

"The way I feel about it today is anything but bold. I'd gladly give you the job, but my editor might not agree."

"That's true," he conceded. "Good luck with the tough one. With both, and don't work too hard."

Her skin tingled where he'd touched her. "Nor you," she said. She should go inside, get her car, and leave. She shouldn't stand there as if waiting for him to kiss her, but his gaze held her pinned, mesmerized. She fought with herself, overcame the desire to stand and chat, to prolong the moment. With firm resolve she said, "Good-bye, Matt."

He bent and brushed a brief kiss over her lips, warm, dry, wholly inadequate, then smiled again and whispered, "See you soon," before he strode off along the sidewalk. Still, Dee stood and watched his back as he headed east until he was lost to sight behind the Sylvia Hotel.

As he walked, Matt considered ways and means of changing Dee's mind. She meant to break contact with him, to refuse to see him again. Of that he was certain. He'd seen that obdurate look in her eyes before, when she was determined to master the art of parallel skiing, or when she intended to pass a difficult exam.

But if there was one thing he'd learned in business, it was that everyone had his price. Or hers. And he already knew what Dee's price was, or one that would at least buy half an hour of her time. The trick would be in finding a source of that particular currency. At Denman Street, he flagged a cab. Taxi drivers were always a good place to start.

It still wasn't working.

Dee shoved her chair back from her computer desk. Her description of the little tree-shaded park tucked in behind city hall wouldn't jell. It didn't help at all that her concentration was off, that she saw Matt's face far more clearly than she saw Captain George Vancouver's, that she heard his voice in the sound of the wind outside, that she wanted, much too intensely, to be with him.

Her doorbell chimed its melodious tune, and she rolled her chair back gratefully. It would only be Jenkins, alerting her that he'd come on duty and was sending back her vegetable basket, but the interruption was welcome.

"Mr. Fiedler to see you, Miss Farris." Her body went almost completely limp for a second as she clutched the back of a chair. "He, um, says it's urgent, miss." Was that a chuckle in Jenkins's normally formal voice?

"I see," she said. "Let me speak to Mr. Fiedler, please, Jenkins."

He spoke before she could even begin to form a coherent thought, a reason to send him away. "Dee . . ." Even through the intercom, his voice had the power to set her heart racing faster. "How's the writing going?"

"It's . . . not." She wasn't absolutely sure why she'd told him the truth. "I finished the easy one. The other just isn't happening."

"Probably because you're hungry," he said, and she wondered, briefly, how he could possibly know she hadn't eaten since that hot dog at lunchtime. "Better let me come up, Dee, before this stuff gets cold."

"What stuff?"

"Smoked meat," he said. "Real, honest-to-goodness smoked-meat sandwiches. Piping hot. Steaming. Begging to be eaten."

Dee's mouth watered. She drew a deep breath. It wasn't possible, but her imagination told her she could actually smell it. Nor was it possible that he had what he claimed. Not here, not this far from the source. "*Montreal* smoked meat?" she asked incredulously.

"The real thing." He sounded smugly self-congratulatory.

He couldn't have . . . Could he? No. Matt wouldn't have been fooled. If he said it was genuine, then it was genuine. But how?

"On rye?" Her voice sounded small and subdued, as if she were begging. She cleared her throat.

"Naturally, on rye."

Dee moaned. "No . . . No, Matt. Don't tease me. It's simply not possible. Go away. I have to work." Lord knew what kind of work she'd turn out now. Gibberish. Maybe she'd surprise and disappoint everyone by writing something banal about the aquarium, which was not her mandate. Everyone wrote about the aquarium!

"Lots of mustard." Matt's insidious voice broke in on her thoughts. "And pickles. These pickles, Dee, must be seen to be believed. And smelled. And tasted. No, not merely tasted, savored." Oh, Lord! Did she hear his teeth actually crunch into a pickle? Imagination again, of course. Why couldn't she apply that imagination to the task she should be doing? "And the sandwiches . . ." he went on. "The meat's piled six inches high. Mmm-mmm! They smell good. Don't they, Jenkins?"

"If Miss Farris doesn't care to partake of hers, sir . . ."

"Oh, she does, Jenkins. She's just playing coy. I tell you, Dee, *Dunn's* couldn't do better than these smoked-meat sandwiches."

At this mention of Montreal's most famous purveyor of smoked meat, she moaned again. "I think I hate you, Matthew Fiedler. Jenkins, send him up, please."

Five minutes later Matt wiped a dribble of juice off his chin and grinned at Dee. "Good, huh?"

"Mmm . . ." She closed her eyes and . . . savored. "Where did you get these?" She examined the plain white paper bags they'd come in. Not a hint of a name or an address or a phone number. Dammit, shouldn't someone who made something this delicious advertise?

"Who's the magician who makes them?" she asked. "And how in the world did you find the real thing in only a few hours, when I've been searching and sampling and rejecting for five years?"

He shook his head, grinning wickedly. "Sorry. Classified information. Just enjoy."

She stared at him as he took a long draft of his beer, draining his glass and setting it down on his place mat. "You can't mean that!" she said. "You wouldn't be so cruel as to keep it a secret from me! Matt, I live here! It's my right as a resident of this city to know. I *have* to know!"

He was unmoved. "No, you don't. As long as I know, and you don't, you'll have to rely on me to supply you. As I said before, I plan to be on the West Coast frequently from now on. How about I bring you one of these each time I arrive?"

She sighed and picked up the last slivers of shaved meat from her plate. "You're a cruel man, Fiedler. Come on, tell me!"

He shoved his chair back and stood, stacking his plate on hers. "Nope." With another grin he sat back down. "That kind of information must be protected. Why, if I told you, a part-time journalist, no less, you'd feel obliged to write a column about it. Talk about your unsung treasures! Then everyone would know. Everyone would go there. And it would simply become another fast-food restaurant serving the masses. McSmoked on McRye. Can you imagine it?"

All too well, she could. Dee shuddered. "And now," she said, "this part-time journalist has a column to write."

"And now," Matt echoed her, "this part-time researcher gets to his real reason for being here." He pulled several sheets of folded, lined yellow paper from his shirt pocket and slapped them onto the table in front of Dee.

"What's this?"

"Research," he said, his face eager. "Go ahead. Read it."

Curious, she unfolded the papers, scanning the first one quickly. Then, more slowly, she read Matt's notes again and moved on to the second sheet, and the third. Filled with facts and figures and interesting anecdotes about Captain George Vancouver, whose statue stood in the park she wanted to write about, they didn't exactly form an article but did provide an excellent basis for one. Assuming she was writing a column on historical figures. Which, regrettably, she was not.

"Matt . . ." She looked up into his expectant face. "You . . . amaze me. Where did you get all this information?"

He didn't respond to that. "It's a moody little place, isn't it?" he asked.

"Yes." Dee frowned. "And it's that mood that I've been trying to capture. I don't see—"

"No wonder," Matt cut in. He grinned. "It's hard to

see anything through the litter of squashed cigarette butts and pigeons scrabbling for handouts, pooping on poor George."

She wrinkled her nose. "Poor George, indeed. What about poor Dee, without a submission for her poor editor? Even if I fail to mention those cigarette butts and the pigeon poop, concentrate on the moss and the fog-dewed spiderwebs spangling the shrubs, the unexpected hush of the place, and that intriguing expression on the captain's face, it doesn't come across as anything more than description. That's not what I'm after. It's just so very hard to express the kind of mood a place like that generates."

She tapped his neatly penned pages on the edge of the table. "And while I'm grateful to you for wanting to help, I have to say that this isn't what I'm after either."

"Are you sure?" he challenged her. "Think about it, Dee. Maybe what I dug up for you is exactly what you need. You're right, it *is* hard to express something so nebulous as mood.

"Each individual sees—feels—atmosphere differently, no matter how alike they are, or how closely attuned. Yet you're trying to show strangers what you *feel* about that particular place, instead of giving them a reason to go there and develop their own liking for it, the way you did with that little pastry place you wrote about last week and the trail under the bridge you told me about today."

"You read my last column?" She was touched to know

that he'd taken the time to search out a copy of *The Bugle* from the previous week.

He shrugged. "Sure. Why not? I wanted to see what kind of work you do.

"And I went to the park, like I said, to see if I could figure out what it was you liked about it, and why you were having problems getting it down on paper. I have a theory."

She had to smile. She remembered how intent he used to get when he wanted to "figure things out."

"Okay. Let's hear your theory."

"I think that Captain George, standing staring off into the distance, is the one who contributes most to the ambience of the place. He doesn't look eager, as an explorer should, but melancholy. Moody. Maybe it's his mood you're picking up on. That got me wondering about him, a man who'd spent his adult life exploring and charting and discovering, a man without a home, or with one he saw only rarely."

Matt rose, his chair legs scraping on the ceramic floor tiles. He paced to the tall windows overlooking the bay, stood gazing out at the squiggles of light reflected in the rumpled water.

"What motivated him?" he asked, turning back. "What pushed him to the farthest reaches of the world?"

He strode back toward Dee, his brows drawn together, shading his eyes. "And I thought about something else: What about the artist who created that statue? Were we sensing his mood, too, somehow?"

As Matt paced, Dee saw a remnant of the intense young man he had been, the one who had planned a life defending the defenseless. She could see him striding about a courtroom, winning over a jury. He strode about her dining alcove now, winning her over with all too much ease.

"I asked myself, had that sculptor understood something about Vancouver, the man, that most historians had missed?" he said. "That got me wondering. How must an explorer, who had set out with such high hopes, feel when he finally admits to himself that he's going to have to tell his superiors that the Northwest Passage doesn't exist? Did he see himself as a failure? His life as wasted?

"I started thinking that if your readers knew who he really was, what his days had been like, he might come more into focus. I don't mean write about the dry facts everyone gets in school, but details, anecdotes, quotations from his journals. Make him more than another bronze statue covered with pigeon crap. Make people see him with new eyes, consider him in a different light. Make them want to go there and see for themselves what you saw in his face, what I did, what that sculptor wanted us to see."

"Yes . . ." Dee said, catching Matt's excitement. A smile broke out on her face as she got to her feet, unfolding the papers again and reading them quickly. "Of course that would work." She looked from the pages to him. "Matt, I think you've just saved my life."

He stepped in close. "Really? Then won't that mean it belongs to me?" He cradled her face in one hand, brushed a kiss across her mouth. She held in the shudder of pleasure that tried to force its way to the surface.

"Matt . . ." Her tone was warning.

His voice was faintly mocking. "Dee . . ."

His eyes laughed, but under that she saw stark, aching need and longed to give in to it. For both their sakes. Her hand shook as she reached up and ran it along his smooth jaw. Under her other hand his arm quivered, but he didn't move, didn't try to make her decisions.

He simply . . . waited.

"I have a column to write," she said again. "And this time, thanks to you, maybe it will actually get done. If you really want to help."

He filched the pages of notes from her hand and held them behind his back. "First, agree to one thing. If we get your column written to printable stage in one hour or less, we spend the balance of the evening together. And have breakfast together tomorrow morning."

She laughed. "That's two things."

Matt leered and twirled an imaginary mustache. "Only if you insist."

"Don't push me too far, Fiedler." She was stern, but she'd had to work at it. She should work as hard at getting him out of there, but she really didn't want to. So what if she knew that the recalcitrant article would never get whipped into shape in less than one hour? She'd anticipated another three, two at the very least. So, what did she have to lose? She hadn't been getting anywhere, sitting in front of her screen thinking about Matt. Maybe if she spent an hour with him, she'd be more able to settle down and do some work when he was gone.

She wished she could believe that.

"All right. One hour. However, I decide when it's printable," she stipulated. "Not you."

Matt grinned. "One hour," he said. He turned her hand over and slapped the material onto her palm. "There you are, my lady. One column, ready to write. Simply add Dee's own special words and touches, stir, and print." Then, leaning close, he said softly, "Now hurry up and get it committed to paper, because you promised once that's done, this evening is ours."

Dee folded her hand around the papers and met his gaze. "All right. But if the evening is 'ours,' doesn't that mean I should have as much say as you in the way we spend it?"

Matt looked wary, but he nodded. "How do you want to spend it?"

"Talking," she said. "Just talking. I give you an hour for my column, you give me an hour of communication."

He stepped back from her. "What about?"

"Matthew Fiedler," she said. "His life and times. Details of his days, anecdotes from his journals. All of those little things, Matt, that help to bring people into focus."

His brows drew together. "You're using my words against me."

She shook her head. "Not against you, Matt. Believe me, I'm not your enemy, and I hold nothing against you. I forgave you long ago. What I'd like now is to be able to understand what drove you." She searched his gaze. "We both agree, I think, that there are certain . . . feelings unresolved between us."

He nodded, his eyes unhappy.

"I think we need to work them out," she said softly. "I want—I need—to know who you are and why you did . . . certain things."

"No." Matt closed his eyes for a second, blocking out Dee's face, her blue, pleading eyes. Then he faced her determinedly. "Be honest, Dee. It's not 'certain things.' It's one thing. My leaving you."

"Yes."

Every part of him resisted what she asked of him. She wanted him to bare his soul to her. He had never done that with anyone. He didn't think he could. "My father was sick."

"That was the excuse, Matt. Not the reason. And until I know what it was, know who you are, I won't be able to understand why you left the way you did."

"You do know who I am," he said tautly. "Or you did."

"I thought I did." Dee rolled the papers into a tight tube. "Obviously, I was wrong. And the man I knew has surely changed in the time we've been apart. How can I know in what way, and how much, unless you tell me?"

"Tell you!" he said explosively. "Tell you what? I was born during a snowstorm in March, I had measles, chicken pox, mumps, and a brother before I started school, and another two brothers later. I skipped third grade. The year I was nine, I broke my leg sliding down an icy hill. I fell in love with Sandra Mandley when I was thirteen, and fell out of love with her when I was fourteen. I enrolled at McGill under a scholarship when I was eighteen. When I was twenty-one, my mother died, and I stopped spending summers at home. I held a part-time job for the remainder of my time at McGill, got good marks despite that, and met a young woman when I was in my senior year. I fell in love. My father became ill, and I was needed at home, so I left Montreal and never saw the young woman again. And there you have it. The life and times of Matthew Fiedler.

"Now, shall we get on with what we're supposed to be doing?"

He saw her patience snap, saw fury leap into her eyes, red patches stain her cheeks. "Dammit, Matt, I'm serious about this. When I was young, I let you shut me out. Now you're the one who wanted in here tonight. You're the one who said we both deserve a chance to get to know each other all over again. How can I get to know you if you refuse—"

He clenched his fists as he took one pace that planted him over her. "Yes, I wanted in tonight. Yes, I want to spend time with you. But why should we waste that time rehashing my childhood, which has no bearing on the present?"

She was in no way intimidated. "Rehashing it?" she said. "I've never heard more than a dozen words about it!"

"You heard enough." He propped his fists on his hips. "You knew I was poor, Dee. I never made a secret of it. I knew you were rich, though at first you did make a secret of that. But because you'd been gently reared, you came clean."

He shook his head. "Why can't you accept that we have enough information about each other's childhoods? Why can't we start building on the basis of what's happening now, and see where this . . . whatever it is . . . takes us?"

"Because that's not good enough for me, Matt! I need more than that."

He slid the tips of his fingers along her lower jaw, into her hair, around the back of her neck. He tilted her face up and brushed his lips over her cheeks, touched her mouth much too briefly, feeling the trembling that told him she needed more than the words she demanded, needed more than she was willing to accept without them.

If he took what he knew she had to give, gave what he knew she wanted as badly as he did, would she forget about the rest of it?

He hesitated, caught between conscience and desire, then stepped back. "I don't know if I have more than that to give you, Dee."

"I think you do."

He gave her a long, level look, then glanced at the lined yellow papers twisted in her hand. "Why do I get such a strong feeling that maybe I should take my research and run?"

Dee's gaze held steady on his. "I don't know, Matt. Why do you think you do? But those are my terms. Take them or leave them."

They stood, three feet apart, looking at each other until he said, "Shall we get to work?"

FIVE

"Done!" Dee rolled her chair back from her desk, this time in triumph.

Matt swiveled her to face him and glanced at his watch. "And in ten minutes short of the hour."

She smiled into his eyes as she stretched and rolled her shoulders to ease the tension. "For that I'll even offer you dessert."

He cocked one brow as he pulled her to her feet. "Dessert?" he asked, slowly running his gaze over her face until it lay warmly on her lips.

They tingled. She touched them with her tongue. Matt's eyes darkened. He turned her and lifted her hair aside to massage her shoulders. "Mmm," she said. "Feels good."

"Mmm," he agreed as he slid his hands into the scooped neck of her sweater and worked his fingers over her muscles. Dee sighed. Her skin tingled, warmed, burned. She planted her hands on the top of her desk, letting her head fall forward. A deep shudder coursed through her body. The hard strength of his fingers worked their magic, and she made another soft sound of appreciation. When she felt the warmth of his breath on her neck, then the brush of his lips on her skin, she tingled all over with a surge of desire.

"Matt . . . Dessert?"

When he lifted her, she leaned back against his chest, enjoying his heat, the feel of his strength. His hands lay flat on the sides of her waist, holding her lightly. "What kind of dessert?" he murmured.

"Ice cream," she whispered. His palms slid upward, to just under her breasts. She felt as if she might sink down to the floor. Would he follow? "With . . . three kinds of . . . syrup," she said.

He turned her to face him, hands linked behind her back. "Three? What are the choices?" He bent his head and nipped at the soft skin just below her ear.

"Butterscotch."

He nuzzled his face into her hair.

"Chocolate . . ." It came out on a sigh he caught and drank in as he brushed his lips over hers. She parted them as her eyelids grew heavier, her body warmer; her heart beat faster, wanting more. She made an effort to keep her eyes open. "Or . . . raspberry."

He slid his hands down her back, cupped her buttocks,

and pulled her against him. He smiled, his lashes at half-mast. "Make mine chocolate *and* raspberry, and you've got yourself a man."

Dee smiled, leaning back in his embrace, aware of the hardness of his body as it pressed against the softness of hers. There was a rightness in the sensations that threaded through her. "And what if I don't want one?" she asked.

His smile faded. "Dee . . . I think you've got one anyway."

She laid her hand on his cheek. "What . . . what am I going to do with him?" At her touch he sucked in a sharp breath. Need leapt into his face, turning it gaunt for a moment. His hands, sliding up her back to tangle in her hair, trembled.

"I wish . . ."

"Me too," she whispered. Oh, Lord! She wished for so much, needed so much. Needed . . . "Matt . . ."

She pulled his head down, placed her parted lips against his, and touched his lower one with the tip of her tongue. "Oh, Matt . . ."

His chest heaved in what might have been, in a different man, a sob. His hard, compelling mouth took over the kiss she'd started, demanding far more than she thought she could give him; his hands begged; his body beseeched.

He stroked her face with his lips, with his fingertips, with his cheek. He'd shaved just to come to her that evening. She smelled his soap, his skin. His breath surged hot and moist against her throat, in her ear as he murmured her name. Her arms encircled his neck, fingers stroking through his hair, rediscovering the textures of it, of him. She breathed in his essence and closed her eyes against the stinging tears that threatened. Tears for the lost past, the unattainable future, but most of all for the sweetness of the present moment.

As if dancing a slow, sensuous dance, they moved of one accord to the sofa. He lowered her to it, followed her down, his weight resting on her, his hips pressing between her thighs.

When he again covered her mouth with his, she sighed tremulously and gave herself over to the exquisite sensations of being in his arms. She trembled. It was too much, too uncontrollable, what was happening to her. She wanted it to stop as much as she wanted it to go on.

Then, as if he knew the precarious state of her emotions, he broke the kiss but held her head in his hands, keeping her face titled toward his as he tunneled his hands through her hair. She drew her lips along his throat and up under his chin, feeling the rasp of whiskers. Oh, Lord, how much she had missed him. She tasted his skin delicately. And this. The taste of him, the feel of his hard body.

When lovemaking hadn't been as intense with Gavin, she'd told herself that it was because she was older, that sex was no longer new and mysterious, a thrilling foreign territory to be explored with eagerness. She'd convinced herself that it wasn't because of any lack in Gavin, or in her, or in the quality of their relationship.

She closed her eyes. Clearly, Gavin had known better.

"Look at me," Matt's voice rumbled.

She opened her eyes, and Matt gazed into them. He sighed and twisted a curl of her hair around his finger as he studied her. He drew the tip of the tress across her lips. "If we don't stop now, Dee, we won't stop at all."

She nodded. "I know."

He sat up. Dee did the same, bending to pick up a gold satin cushion that had tumbled to the floor. An aching yearning still pulsed through her, and she clutched the cushion to her middle.

"I made you a promise. I don't want to break it. I've done too much of that in my life."

For a long moment both were silent, looking at each other in the wake of that statement. "Matt . . . I understand."

He shook his head as he got to his feet. "No. I don't think you do. And I think you're right. It's time you did."

Dee rose. "I made you a promise, too, didn't I? Ice cream. With chocolate and raspberry syrups."

Bowls before them, they sat again at the round oak dining table. Matt took a spoonful and ate it slowly, looking anywhere but at Dee. After several more bites he shot her a glance from under his brows. She sat there waiting, calm, her face serene, her gaze clear. He cleared his throat. "I don't know," he said.

Dee kept her voice soft, quiet. "Don't know what?" It hurt her to see Matt was suffering. Maybe she should just let this go, let things happen as they would naturally. Maybe in time he would open up to her, let her in. Making love . . . that was communication, wasn't it? Couldn't that lead to the kind of closeness she dreamed of sharing with Matt? How could she go on bearing the look of torture in his eyes, torture her demands had put there?

"Matt . . ."

"I don't know," he said again, "how to go about this. I mean, where do I even start telling someone like you something like my life? My childhood. It wasn't interesting. And it certainly wasn't noble. It was . . . drudgery. Something to be gotten through. A day at a time. It was . . . gray, Dee. That's what I remember most about my life before McGill. It was simply colorless."

Someone like her? That hurt. He was still making differences between them, still keeping her apart, as if what she felt, what he felt, offered no hope of bringing them together.

"I don't want to be entertained," she said. "I want to be informed. Let me have it. You gave me the journal of Captain Vancouver. Now give me the journal of Matthew Fiedler."

Still he resisted, his mouth tight, his fists clenched, but then he nodded. "All right. As long as you remember it's Matthew Fiedler, Esquire, of Metcom, Inc., not Captain Fiedler, intrepid explorer of the Royal Navy."

He sat silent for a minute or two, stirring his half-melted ice cream before going on. "My life's been mostly a bore, Dee, not one of excitement and discovery. The only thing I share with your old sea dog is disappointment, maybe even a sense of failure because I never found my elusive Northwest Passage either."

"And what was that?"

He fixed his gaze on her. "You know the answer, Dee."

She did. His storefront law office. Defending the defenseless. Freeing the oppressed. That was what he had wanted then. Too much time had passed. Maybe they no longer remembered things the same way. She shook her head. "No. I want you to tell me."

He took several long, slow spoonfuls before replying heavily, sounding almost annoyed at being pressed for an answer. "You were, of course. You were what I wanted and couldn't have. Couldn't . . . find."

Her throat ached. Her chest felt tight. "I was there, Matt. All along. You knew that. You had only to come to me."

He shoved his bowl aside. "I don't mean it literally. I meant I knew I couldn't find a way to have you, to keep you. So I left. To give us both a chance to find . . ." He slid his glance back to her face. "To find whatever we could . . . have."

She met his gaze and held it. "And what did you find, Matt, that you 'could' have?" She drew in a deep breath and let it out, remembering that he had been fingering a satin negligee when she'd first set eyes on him Monday morning. Might as well get all the answers at the same time. "Who?"

His eyes widened, startled. He hadn't expected that question, she saw. "No one."

"Matt . . ." Her tone was reproachful. "You're thirty-six years old."

"All right. No one . . . permanent. And certainly not then, not at first. There was no time, and I had no heart for it anyway." He looked at her bleakly. "Hell, Dee, I never wanted to tell you this. I lied to you. I said that I was going home because my dad was sick. He wasn't sick. He'd been fired from his job. All right, yes, he needed me. That much was true."

He drew a deep breath. "But if it hadn't happened, I'd have gone anyway. I was glad for the excuse. I wanted it over between you and me."

She stared at him. "Why couldn't you tell me that?" she asked.

He closed his eyes. "I . . . Lord, Dee! You were so young, so tender, so sweet. No one had ever hurt you before. Hell, I'd taken your virginity. I'd . . . made you love me. Made you vulnerable. And I'd known since I met your parents that it would never work between you and me. Dad's needing me came at an opportune time for me, as hard as it was." He looked down for a minute, then up again. "For everyone. Me too."

She wondered if she should thank him for that acknowledgment, but didn't. The less she talked, the more he would. Besides, her throat hurt too much to force words through it. Her jaws ached. Even her teeth hurt.

"Did I ever tell you how my mother died?"

Dammit, he knew he hadn't! Wordlessly, she shook her head.

"She died of a lifetime of overwork. Overwork and despair. They called it cancer, but that was the symptom, not the real disease. In addition to raising her children and keeping her own house spotless, she worked as a waitress during the day, then turned out and cleaned the mining-company offices every evening.

"She did this not for luxuries, not even to keep on top of the ever-present bills, but in the hope of getting ahead. That was her bottom line. To get ahead." He breathed hard now, too rapidly, and his face had gone pale. "For my sake."

Dee reached out and touched the back of his hand, then spoke his name.

As if her touch was painful, he recoiled from it, rubbing his hand where her fingers had lain. "The money she saved was meant to give *me* a chance," he went on. "Me, the eldest by five years, because she believed that if I got out, got an education, then I'd be able to help the others do the same.

"So she worked, and saved, and told me repeatedly that when I had my education, I would go to work for a man named Edwin James. He was a shirttail relative of hers. I think they'd once had crushes on each other. At any rate he'd promised her faithfully that if she ever needed anything, she was to come to him. Or if anyone of hers had a need, he'd see to it. To this end she was determined to see me educated.

"But each time she thought she had it made, there'd be a worldwide drop in the price of coal, and it wasn't profitable for the company to keep running. So they'd lay off the men, often for months, and a couple of times for a year or more. That meant the café's business fell off, and Mom's day job was gone. With only a skeleton staff in management, they didn't need her to clean offices, and when the unemployment insurance ran out, we'd go on welfare. Dad would drink more, he'd stay out late, get into fights, take up with women.

"Each time that happened, my mom got a little bit thinner, a little more tired, a little more despairing. We couldn't leave. The grocery store, Mandley's, was company-backed. We owed them money. Our house was a company house. We couldn't afford the rent anywhere else, assuming my father could have found work. Coal mining was all he knew, all his father and grandfathers had known for a long way back.

"But Mom always said that I'd be the one to break the cycle. *I'd* be a man of importance, a man in a three-piece suit, like the legendary Edwin James. I'd make decisions for others to carry out. When she said that, her eyes would shine. Her face would take on an almost holy look. Her hope, she called me. Her children's door into the future. If I could escape from the circle of debt and despair endured by all the generations that had gone before us, if I could get out before my face was lined with care and tattooed with coal dust and get my brothers to follow, then she could die, unashamed for once in her life.

"Unashamed." He leaned forward, shaking his bowed head between his hands. "My mother lived with shame, and I never fully knew it." He lifted his gaze. "Until I was the one who shamed her."

"That day she told me how she had to fight to hold her head up when everyone knew that my father drank and was unfaithful. She'd managed to appear grateful for charity and proud at the same time. She'd never let on to her children how ashamed she was of the life she'd brought us into."

"But none of it was her fault," Dee protested. "Couldn't she see that?"

"No. No, she couldn't. There *is* terrible disgrace in being on welfare, Dee. You'll never know it. Never understand. Even in a town where nearly everyone else is in the same straits, there's a stigma you can't erase."

Dee saw remembered humiliation on his face, in the eyes he had to force to meet hers.

"One day she sent me to the store to buy a cake mix and candles because it was Ronnie's fifth birthday. He's the youngest. Mr. Mandley refused to put them on my parents' tab. He said people like us couldn't afford luxuries like cake."

Matt's jaw clenched. "And Sandra Mandley, my girlfriend, was right there. She heard me ask. She heard her father's reply. She was a witness to my humiliation, and I hated her for that. Because fourteen-year-old boys aren't always rational, I hated her even more when she sneaked over to our house later with a cake mix and candles and offered them to us as a gift.

"I threw her out, and her cake mix with her. I have never felt such rage, such bitterness, or such helplessness. I . . . didn't conduct myself like a gentleman, a capital crime in my mother's eyes. She always said that we might be poor, we might have patches, but we were from a good home and should act accordingly. If we didn't, we shamed her."

He ran a hand into his hair. "I shamed her, all right. That night I broke into the store. I trashed the place with a baseball bat. You can do a surprising amount of damage in ten minutes. Thousands and thousands of dollars' worth. I didn't get caught."

His voice shook. "Nobody would even have suspected me. I was a good kid, you see. I got great marks in school. I had *potential*. I was a town favorite."

He buried his face in his hands for a moment, then thrust his shoulders back and looked at Dee squarely. "But my mother knew. As soon as the news was out, she knew. She confronted me, and I confessed to her. She cried. I had never seen my mother cry like that." Tears sheened his eyes as if the pain of that remembered scene was too much to bear, but he continued to face her and went on.

"She didn't cry for long. She took her savings out of the quart sealers where she'd hidden them. That was the first time I ever knew of their existence, the first time I had some inkling that her plans for me were more to her than an idle dream. There were eight of those sealers that she'd stuffed over the years with the lousy tips she got in the restaurant, hoarded dollar by dollar, with odds and ends of what she could sneak away from other family needs. She couldn't put her money in a bank because of the times we had to go on welfare. Welfare people can't have savings like that, not openly. And somehow, she'd managed to keep my dad from finding it when he was on his binges.

"She marched me over to Mandley's store. I had to confess to him, to throw myself on his mercy. She said that if he chose to tell the company, which she knew would press charges and probably fire my father, she would still tell the truth in court. She said that no amount of anger and hurt had entitled me to do what I'd done. And of course, she was right. But whatever Mandley's decision, her orders were that I would apologize. And I would use her savings to make restitution."

He stared at a point over Dee's shoulder for several moments. "And she told me that if, due to my actions, I could never live out her dreams for me, that was to be her punishment and mine, for the sin of pride. She hoped that I had learned one lesson that no university could ever teach me: that a man's honor was more valuable than any amount of money, any career, even more important than pride. And if paying off our debt to the company and Mr. Mandley was the price we had to pay to reclaim my honor, then she did it gladly. So we paid 'our' debt. *My* debt. With her money.

"Then she forgave me. She . . . absolved me and said we would go forward from that day. We did. And she never mentioned the incident again, never changed in her attitude toward me. But I had changed.

"When the mine reopened, she went back to her two jobs and started saving again. I got a job, too, oddly enough working for Mandley, sweeping floors and dusting shelves, and when I had worked off the family's tab, I started saving to pay my mother back.

She called it 'saving for my tuition.' I called it paying her back. I didn't want to use it. I was lucky enough to get that scholarship, but she insisted that the savings go toward my living expenses that the scholarship didn't cover, so that I wouldn't have to 'waste' study time on a job. But summers I went back to Mandley's."

Including that summer he had left her? "And Sandra?"

He smiled without humor. "Sandra got pregnant when she was seventeen and married a guy we used to call

Dennis the Dink. He's a day-shift foreman in the mine now, and they have three kids. Sandra works mornings in her father's store and cleans the elementary school in the evenings."

His expression told her he thought he'd had a lucky escape. "No, I went back summers to be with my mother. She had breast cancer. She kept saying she had it licked. She didn't. She might have if she'd had some reserves left to fight it with, but she was too thin, too tired, too . . . beaten. The year before I met you, she died. And she made me promise to stop coming back. She was so afraid, you see, that I'd get trapped there somehow, despite having gone away to school."

He'd said he'd broken 'too many' promises. "But . . . you did go back?" Or had that part of it been a lie too?

He nodded. "It's funny. I know a few people who had alcoholic parents. The usual thing is to condemn them, hate them. Yet I could never hate my dad. I hated what he did, but I loved him. He tried, Dee, but the system beat him down as surely as it did my mother. I was lucky I'd managed to break free of that system, managed to do what she wanted. Otherwise, I might have ended up as defeated as Dad was.

"But then, when he got fired, of course he had to leave his house; it belonged to the company, and without a job, with a drinking problem and two kids still to support, he needed my help."

He leaned forward, his face tense, his voice taut as he

pleaded with her for understanding. "And I could not take you with me, Dee. You were an eighteen-year-old girl from a privileged background. All right, you were nineteen by then," he went on as she tried to speak.

"Your age wasn't important. Your . . . future was. To me. Not only would you have been completely unable to cope with that kind of life, with the poverty, it would have been an insult to my mother and her memory for me to drag any woman into the very life she'd killed herself for me to escape."

Dee stared at him and hugged her arms tight around her middle. "Did you go back and work in the mine?"

He shook his head. "That was my intention, but they weren't hiring. So I moved my father and two youngest brothers to Digby, where Dad's brother lived, and where Colin, the brother next to me, was in trade school. I dropped out of school for a year, worked on my uncle's scallop boat. Somehow, we kept things together."

"Then?" she prompted when he'd stayed silent too long.

"Then my dad quit drinking, joined AA, and he was working again—on the boats. I enrolled in Dalhousie University, got my law degree, passed my bar exams, and went to where the big money was, Toronto, and got a job."

"With Edwin James."

"Right. Edwin James, Metcom, Inc."

Dee looked at him, unsatisfied despite the amount of information he'd provided. "End of story?"

It had only made her hungry for more. What about his dreams? What about the oppressed, the poor, the defenseless? The people such as his parents, she now understood, whom he had wanted to defend. He'd obviously given up those dreams in order to earn enough to help his brothers through school. But Ron, the youngest, must be through college now.

"End of story," Matt said, his tone flat. "Feel you know me better? More to the point, do you like me any better?"

She stood and went to draw the drapes across the windows. "No, Matt."

She didn't know how close he was behind her until he spoke softly. "No to which question?"

She turned and met his steady gaze. "I loved you, you know. And I could have coped with the life—any life—if it meant being with you. It hurts to know that you didn't trust me, trust my—trust the strength of my love."

He blew out a frustrated breath. "Dee . . . come on! You were a kid!"

"Maybe so, but . . ." She turned and strode into the living room, turned on the CD player, not much caring what was on it. Mozart flooded the room.

"But what?"

She spun and faced him. "But you owed me the option of making that decision myself!"

Though he stood half the room away, she saw his eyes flare with anger. His voice rose over throbbing violins. "The hell I did! You say you don't know me now. Well, if you think for one minute I could have let you or any woman make a crazy decision, one based on emotion not sense, you didn't know me even then!" He sucked in a ragged breath, then added, emphasizing each word with a step that brought him closer to her, "You could not have withstood the rigors of that kind of life!"

"Dammit, Matt!" she yelled, slapping her palm on the lid of the piano. "If I was old enough to share your bed, I was old enough to share your life. Your problems. Maybe you never knew me well enough, if you thought I was so shallow that I'd crumble at the first hint of pressure."

"I knew you, Dee. I knew the way you thought, the way you wanted to take on every injustice you saw and make it right. And you'd have failed, because the life I came from, the one I was going back to, was filled with injustices.

"We'd have had a few good months, or a couple of good years, but then the decay would have set in. It was that prospect I couldn't face. The thought of watching you turn bitter and cold, or sad and despairing like my mother. The idea of your coming to hate me was too much for me. And you would have come to hate me, because my pride wouldn't have let me let you use what was rightfully yours to make your own life easier. I knew the man I was then. I know myself now too. If pride is a sin, then I still transgress daily."

Dee cringed. "And there we have it, don't we? When you said your father was ill and you had to leave right away, I made the mistake of offering you money for your flight, so you wouldn't have to take the bus or hitch. That was my unforgivable crime, wasn't it, Matt? It was comparable to wanting to give you a cake and candles for your little brother's birthday."

"Dee . . ."

"All right," she went on. "For that lapse in judgment, I apologize. I was wrong. And I admit it was my youth and inexperience that made me do it. But that doesn't mean my lack of years would have made me a bad wife for you. If you had simply told me I'd hurt your feelings by offering money as a solution to your problems, I would have understood. I wasn't stupid, Matt, just naive."

"Hurt my—" He broke off, rammed a hand through his hair, and closed his eyes for a moment, breathing hard. "Dee! For the love of God! Do you think it was just my feel—" Again he cut himself off in midword. He blew out a long breath. "Oh, dammit, this is not the way I intended for us to spend this evening, dragging up the pains of years past and yelling at each other as a result."

He stared at her until his breathing subsided to normal levels. He pinched the bridge of his nose and squinted as if his eyes hurt him. "I did what I thought was right, what I saw then as the only thing I could do. You were who you were. I was who I was. And the time wasn't right for us. A clean break was best."

She nodded, weariness overcoming her.

What, after all, had changed? She was still who she was. And Matt clearly still had his pride. Whatever he might want from her, she was sure it was nothing permanent. "Yes," she said. "A clean break. Then. As now."

His scowl deepened. "That's crazy. You're punishing me for the past."

She shook her head. "No. I realized that the past is something that can never be changed, never be rebuilt. What we had we lost."

She was tempted to say, *You threw it away*, but that wouldn't be fair. There was blame on both sides. More, probably, on hers than on his. She hadn't been honest with him about herself. She'd wanted a "real boyfriend" like other girls had had since they were a lot younger than she'd been when she met Matt.

She hadn't told him who her father was, what he did, or about her family's wealth. She'd been afraid—rightly— that it would get in the way.

Nor had she told him she was a virgin.

He'd always been so damned *honorable*. She understood that better now. The second he knew he was Dee's first lover, he'd been convinced he should marry her.

Then, once he'd learned what kind of background she came from, he'd been equally convinced that he should not. Could not. For a time she thought she'd persuaded him he was wrong. And then he'd left. Now, she knew, willingly.

"For three years I waited, Matt. I couldn't believe that you'd . . . abandoned me. Abandoned what we had. I thought you'd really loved me."

"Ah, Dee! I did love you. And I didn't want to leave you like that. I simply had no choice."

Matt wished he could tell her how difficult it had been. He wished he could explain how much he had loved her. He wanted to tell her he knew he could fall in love with her all over again, very, very easily. That maybe he had already, and again he didn't want to leave her, not for even a minute. "I could—" He clamped his mouth shut, staring at her delicate oval face, drinking in her beauty. Behind her, around her, the aura of wealth still lay as a barrier between them. But did it have to be an impenetrable one? Especially since it was all of his own making?

"You could what?" she asked.

"I could . . . imagine your father's reaction to my asking him for you," he said. "It scared the hell out of me."

"But . . ." His heart hammered hard, high in his chest, in his throat. Her father was gone now. He wouldn't have to ask. He could do, now, what he'd done long ago before he knew she even had a father, simply take what she offered so sweetly, so innocently. She looked at him, questions in her eyes. She didn't invite him to continue what he'd been going to say.

The grandfather clock wheezed and bonged twelve times. Both turned to look at it, as if it might have some of the answers they lacked.

"It's late. I should go."

Dee said, "Yes. It's late. Later for you than for me. Your body must still be on eastern time."

He let his gaze rest on her averted profile. "I adjust easily." He waited a heartbeat or two. She didn't turn. Didn't suggest that he stay. Or that he return. When she moved, it was toward the foyer.

He waited as she got his coat out of the closet and handed it to him. He shrugged into it. She slid open the glass door and held the bead curtain aside. Birds murmured sleepily about humans who kept ridiculous hours.

At the elevator Matt took both Dee's hands in his. "Good night," he said softly. Their evening was over. He knew that. Still, he found it hard to let go of her hands.

It was possible, too, that she was right, and their entire relationship was over, had been over for thirteen years. That he was trying to recapture something that existed only in memory, like hoping for the sweet new scent of summer in the faded photograph of a rose.

No. He rejected that notion. "Maybe we can't rebuild the past," he said. "But what about starting fresh?"

Again she looked at him silently for several moments. With a smile so sad, it made him want to weep, she said, "Good night, Matt."

Matt stepped into the elevator, and the brighter light

there shone down onto his face, glancing off the hard planes and angles of his bones, the firm, straight line of his mouth. Dee saw with stunning clarity the lost, bleak loneliness almost hidden in the dark shadows beneath his brows. But then the carved doors slid shut, and he was gone.

Dee sat in front of her computer screen, rereading the words she had written with Matt's input. It was a good column, an interesting one, and she could take pride in it. For a moment she let her forehead rest on a fist, remembering. . . .

If pride's a sin, then I still transgress daily. . . . Oh, Matt, Matt.

With a sigh she walked her cursor back to the top, typed in the title, and then, under that, added the words *By Dee Farris.* After a brief pause, she added three more words.

Maybe Matt's mother had instilled in him a sense of honor. Her parents had always believed in giving credit where credit was due.

She turned on her printer and watched the characters leap black across the white of the page.

By Dee Farris and Matthew Fiedler. The names looked good together.

If only she didn't believe that to Matt "starting fresh" meant forgetting the lessons of the past.

SIX

Matt shouldered himself away from the cold of a brick wall, suddenly alert after more than half an hour of bone-chilling, passive waiting, or as passive as a pacing man could be. Across the street Dee and two other women emerged from an anonymous office tower and ran down a flight of broad steps together, one wrapping her arms around herself, shivering exaggeratedly. It was a raw night, with the threat of more rain in the air. A water wall spilled down in a silver shimmer, wind whipping streaks of spray off it to splash the sidewalk.

Dee wore jeans, a down-filled jacket, and white sneakers. Her hands were shoved deep into her pockets. As Matt waited for the light, he saw weariness in her step, a slump to her shoulders. Her hair hung loose, the wind snatching it and dragging it across her eyes. She shoved it back with an ungloved hand.

He crossed the street and came up behind the trio as they approached three cars parked closely together, Dee's Mercedes sports coupe endmost in the row.

"Wait," he said, then cursed himself for a fool, because all three women froze, backs hunched as if waiting for blows. It was only for an instant. The largest of the three spun, arms up in a martial-arts fighting position. Dee's head snapped around. The third woman put the length of a car between herself and Matt. He saw something glint in her hand.

He remembered a woman saying on a TV news program, "It's endemic. The danger's everywhere." And he had thought he knew that, that everyone did. Maybe everyone did on an intellectual level, but no man would ever experience the fear of a woman on a city's streets at night. He saw that fear, stark and elemental, on Dee's face, on the faces of all three.

"Oh, hell," he said. "I'm sorry, kid. Dee . . . I didn't mean to startle you."

The one with the instinctive fighting stance, a head taller than Dee and probably eighty pounds heavier, planted herself between Matt and Dee. "You got a problem, buster?"

"Nancy, it's all right," Dee said, stepping forward quickly. "Matt's a friend." She swept her gaze over his face, looking for clues, finding none.

Nancy hesitated. "You're sure?"

"I'm sure." To reassure her companions, Dee slipped

her fingers through Matt's elbow and felt his arm clamp her hand to his side. "I, uh, forgot he'd be by tonight to meet me," she said. "Good night, Nan. 'Night, Sue."

With a last, suspicious look the other woman entered her car.

Dee waited until both her companions were gone before she snatched her hand out of Matt's arm. "What are you doing here?" she demanded. "How did you know where to find me?" For a man who'd wanted to start fresh, he'd certainly kept himself apart since Tuesday night.

Matt shook his head ruefully, his dark hair wind-tossed, his eyes shadowed. "Would you believe I tailed you when you left your building this evening?" He looked as if he had trouble believing it himself.

She stared at him as she backed up a pace. "*Tailed* me? How?"

He shrugged and stuffed his hands into his coat pockets. "By telling a taxi driver, 'Follow that car.' I told him you were my wife and I wanted to catch you red-handed with your lover. He acted like he didn't believe me. I think he figured I was a cop and you were a crook. I felt like James Bond."

She laughed, but Matt saw little signs of stress around her eyes. "Except Bond would never chase a woman."

"Of course not. He might've used the excuse as cover, though."

"True. But he'd have been more likely to politely put the driver on the sidewalk and commandeer the cab. Then he'd have stood it on two wheels as he slalomed between parked vehicles and garbage cans." They'd watched a lot of Bond movies too.

He nodded. "You're right. I didn't do anything nearly so dramatic. But then, you didn't force me to by trying to lose me."

Her face took on a still, closed look. In the silence between passing cars the water wall hissed and splashed. "I didn't know you were following," Dee said.

"And if you had?"

He heard the lock on her car door snap open and realized she must have a remote control for it. "I . . . don't know," she said. Her gaze was troubled. He opened the door, and she got in, out of the wind, out of the cold. It blew his pant legs tight against his calves. His raincoat flapped around his thighs and knees. He pulled up the collar. She unlocked the passenger side.

"Get in, Matt. I'll take you back to your hotel."

By the time he'd slid into the car, she had the engine running. With both doors shut, the heater soon took care of the chill. "Returning to my hotel wasn't on my agenda," he said. "I came to take you out for a nightcap."

"Matt . . ." Unhappily, Dee met his gaze. "I'm still not sure this is such a good idea."

"No?" he said. Having a nightcap? Seeing each other? He didn't have to ask. He stroked his thumb over the rapid pulse in her throat, took her hand, and slid it inside his coat, holding it over the hammering of his heart. "You got a better one? Some way to make yourself stop thinking about me, the way I've looked for ways to stop thinking about you? Some way to stop the feelings, Dee?"

She didn't try to deny that she'd been thinking of him. She hadn't seen him or heard from him since he'd left her apartment Tuesday night, but he'd been in her mind, in her dreams. She'd gone over and over things he'd said, things she'd said, and spent far too many hours remembering his kisses and how they could turn her inside out.

They exchanged a long look. She glanced down first and pulled her hand away.

"No. No, I guess I don't." It would be so much easier, her life less complex, if he had never appeared in her shop. But since he had, she knew that neither of them was simply going to walk away from this. Not easily, and not soon. And not unharmed. But whatever happened, she knew it wasn't going to be a fresh start. Fresh starts between former lovers were mythical, romantic impossibilities. Always the past would be there between them.

The past they had shared. And the separate pasts they had not.

She sighed. Then, because she couldn't help herself, because it was important to know the answer, she asked, "Why did you follow me?"

In the lights of a passing vehicle she saw his wry smile. "Not to offer you a nightcap. But you figured that out all by yourself, didn't you? I came here to wait for you because I was afraid that even if I could get past the doorman, you wouldn't let me into your elevator. And I needed to see you. I . . . wanted to be a hero. Your hero. I wanted to . . . hold you, when you came out of that horror chamber."

He reached across the console again and took her hand off the wheel, cradling it in his. His fingers were warm, and his grip, though gentle, was strong. This time she didn't pull away. Sensing her compliance, maybe even her need, he tucked her hand between his neck and his palm, inside the warmth of his collar.

After a moment Dee nodded and curled her fingers against his skin. "Thank you, Matt. Everyone who works those phone lines needs a hug when she's done. I'm glad you're here." Her teammates had both gone home to husbands and concern and love. Many times she had envied them that comfort.

"I wish I could put my arms around you," he said, and she felt his voice through her hand as well as heard it in her ears. "Why do you have to drive such a dumb little car?"

"There are those who would take great exception to hearing you describe a Mercedes 380 SL as a 'dumb little car.'"

He grinned. "You one of them?"

She shook her head. "A car's a car. My mother bought me this one for my birthday last year." Something flickered in his eyes. Shock? Disgust? She thought of his mother, saving her restaurant tips, dollar by dollar, in quart sealers that she'd had to hide from not only a drunken husband, but from the welfare people who'd have taken her sons' escape. She thought of how hard-earned Matt's new life was and wondered if it felt precarious to him.

Still, he had to understand that her mother never gave inexpensive gifts. If it was going to be a problem, she wanted to know now.

His focus, though, was elsewhere. "All those things you hear on Thursday nights," he said. "Have they made you hate men?"

Again she shook her head. "No, Matt." She slid her hand farther around his neck, squeezing gently. "And nothing you've ever done has made me hate you."

He closed his eyes momentarily, then looked at her, his face expressionless. "I didn't ask that."

She searched his eyes. "Didn't you?"

He sighed and slid her hand out from under his collar, then set it back on the steering wheel. He gave it a sharp pat. "Nobody likes a know-it-all," he said.

"Matt, I wish you wouldn't worry about the things I hear on Thursday nights. I don't let them cling. The problems aren't my problems. I sympathize. I try not to empathize," She looked at her hands on the wheel, then cast a sidelong glance at Matt. "I think, if I could live my life over, make choices knowing what I know now about myself, I'd have gone into psychology, not journalism."

"There is, though, a certain psychology used in journalism," he said.

Dee nodded and put the car in gear. "Yes, but what I'd really like to do is understand the kind of mind that permits a man to do terrible, violent things to women. There has to be a way to reach such a man, treat him, show him a better way."

He glanced at her. "Not many women have any compassion for rapists."

She shrugged. "I'm not sure I do. But if there's a way to stop its happening, maybe that's the direction we have to start looking."

When she came to a stop in the parking area of a drive-in restaurant after driving several blocks, Matt grinned. "Lord! I haven't been to one of these in years! Do they still have cute little waitresses in short skirts and high boots?"

She laughed and rolled down the window as a male carhop in long pants and a down-filled vest came running over. "It has been years for you, hasn't it?" she said, then asked, "What will you have?"

After they'd ordered hot chocolate, she rolled up the window again.

"What would you do, Matt, if you could live your life over? You went into law to fulfill your mother's dream. Was it yours?"

"Law wasn't necessarily what she wanted for me. Just an education. An avenue of escape. I chose law because I liked the idea of the power I thought it would give me. Power to fix things. But if I could do it over again, I think I'd take architecture. There's even more power in that. The power to create something lasting, something of . . . value."

"Power," she said, smiling. "That's such a male thing to want."

He smiled back at her. "I am male."

Dee nodded. "I've noticed that a time or two. I can see that in working for a corporation heavily into property development, you're helping to create things of lasting value. I'm glad for you about that, Matt."

He drained his cup and licked the foamy mustache off his upper lip. "And I'm glad for you that you can give some of your time to working with people who need what you give them—compassion, sympathy, and, whether you like to admit it or not, empathy."

Dee finished her chocolate and set both cups on the tray outside her window. The boy returned almost at once and smiled at them in thanks for the tip Matt had added to the tab.

At his hotel Matt didn't let the console stop him from doing what he wanted. What Dee wanted. He leaned across it, cupped the back of her head in one hand, and tilted her face up to his. His kiss was warm and deep and wet, sweet with chocolate and his own taste. It stirred her to the depths. It made her head spin and her heart race and her breath catch in her throat.

"Good night, kid," he said, smiling into her eyes. "I'll be in touch. I—"

Whatever else he'd meant to say he bit off as he clamped his teeth shut and shouldered his way out of her car. He slammed the door on her and murmured, "Good night."

As he strode toward the gilt-trimmed main-entrance doors, she flung her door open and jumped out, calling his name.

Matt's heart nearly stopped at the sound of Dee's voice. He turned. She stood with her elbows on the roof of her car, her head tilted to one side. The wind played in her hair, tumbling it. Light from a neon sign across the street backlit it, creating a halo effect. He couldn't read her expression, but he saw her chest rise as she drew in a deep breath.

It was as if she had strings attached to his ankles, he thought, discovering that his feet were in motion. He returned to her car, stood leaning on the roof from the other side.

"*Friday the Thirteenth* is playing in a theater not far from where I live," she said. "It's for the one night only. Friday."

"The thirteenth," he said, then waited for her to continue. "Is that going to be my lucky day?" he asked when she did not.

She knew, in inviting him, that she was agreeing to that fresh start he wanted. That she wanted too. What she didn't know was if it would work. But how could she not agree? How could she not take the risk? That was Matt standing there waiting for her to say what she had to say. Matt . . . who would never go away, no matter how many miles or years they put between them.

"Would you . . . would you like to come and have an early dinner with me, then go see it?"

He smiled. "Lady, you've got yourself a date."

Then, as she ducked back into her car and shut the door, he stood back and watched her drive away. He closed his eyes. Tomorrow Metcom and Chang International were to sign the final agreement on the property purchase that included the Westmarch Apartment Hotel. Undoubtedly, there'd be a celebration dinner afterward, speeches, toasts, the whole boring routine.

He wondered how he was going to talk Edwin into letting him off the hook.

As luck had it, his boss and the CFO were coming out of a bar as he entered the lobby. They chatted for several moments before Marcy excused herself, saying that tomorrow was going to be a long and busy day, thus presenting him with the perfect lead-in.

"Not at all, my boy!" Several whiskey-sodas had likely added to Edwin's expansiveness, and the thought of a successful conclusion to their main matter of business wouldn't be hurting either. "As a matter of fact, I was going to suggest that you head on home tomorrow. Have a bit of R and R. After all, you were here a week longer than the rest of us. You deserve a break."

"Thanks, Edwin. If you're sure you won't need me? And if you don't mind, I won't be checking out tomorrow. I have a date for the evening and . . ." He hesitated. "I'm not yet sure about the weekend."

"You sly dog, you. In town less than two weeks and already you've found yourself a squeeze." Edwin liked to talk what he thought was "modern." "Yes, yes. You keep your room." He nudged Matt with an elbow. "Maybe bring the lady by to meet your boss. Give you a good excuse to get her into the hotel. Then it would be a simple matter to 'need' to fetch something from your room and . . ." He smiled slyly. "You know the routine."

Matt nodded, feeling slightly sick. The "routine" was not something Dee would appreciate.

He left Edwin, his mind fully occupied with Dee. As the elevator rose, he saw in the mirrored wall before him the size of his smile. It fit his face. It felt fine there. The only thing that would have made it feel better was knowing that his date the next night wouldn't be the last one.

It was nice to be dressing for a date with Matt, even if it was only for a movie. Her second date in as many years, Dee thought. And both with the same man, both in the same week. She stood before the pier glass in her bedroom, fastening a gold link belt around her waist over the top of her thigh-length pale yellow cashmere sweater. She smoothed the sweater over the hips of her black skirt and sat on the edge of her bed to pull on high, soft leather boots.

Matt was coming to her home again. He'd sit at her table, eat food she'd grown and prepared. Would he have read her column in *The Bugle*? It had been on the stands since early that morning. She'd asked the editor to run the article Matt had helped with first so she could enjoy his reaction to their shared byline. Excitement rippled through her, excitement she couldn't suppress. Sharing things with Matt felt so good!

Out in the solarium the macaw shrieked, and Dee forgot all about weekly newspapers, columns, and by-lines. Matt was there. *Matt* . . .

"That," Matt said, grinning as Dee swept aside the bead curtain to admit him to her apartment, "has got to be the most distinctive doorbell I've ever heard. Or is he your watch bird?"

"Take your pick," she said, leading the way inside. "Here, give me your coat. Is it still raining?"

"What else would it be doing?" he asked.

She shot him a reproachful look. "Now, really. Remember Tuesday? And yesterday? Did it rain then?"

He had to admit it had not, but it was fun teasing her, making her eyes sparkle.

"Your cooking," he said half an hour later, twirling spaghetti around his fork, "has improved considerably."

Dee smiled at him. "Thank you. Has yours?"

"Mine?" He paused with his fork halfway to his mouth. "There was nothing wrong with mine. I taught you, remember?"

"You taught me scrambled eggs, Matt. And pizza from a package. Tacos, too, if I recall. And that ain't cookin'."

He roared with laughter. "You shouldn't even try to use words like 'ain't' or drop your terminal *g*'s. It just sounds silly, coming from you. And what would your elocution teacher say?"

"I never had an elocution teacher," she said, her chin tilting haughtily. "I never required one."

He grinned. "No. I don't suppose you did. You come by that snooty accent naturally, don't you? Though it's getting a tad blurred around the edges." He sipped his wine and looked at her over the rim of his glass, sobering.

"For a long time I used to dream of your voice. I'd wake up still hearing it." What he didn't say was, *and want to cry.* Once or twice, when he'd been too tired to maintain full control, he had cried.

"Matt . . ." Her gaze searched his face then she shook her head. Yes, they'd talk about all those intervening years. But not now. "Eat your dinner. The movie starts in less than an hour."

As they tiptoed around puddles on the wet sidewalk, huddled together under an umbrella that kept neither of them dry, Matt said, "And it wasn't scrambled either. It was omelets. Big, beautiful, fat omelets filled with all sorts of good things. Mushrooms, cheese, onions, olives, bacon, bologna, whatever I could think of. Remember?"

Dee swallowed against the ache in her throat. She remembered. She remembered far too much, far too well. It was all coming back in such powerful waves, she wondered if she'd survive the evening.

The movie. She'd concentrate on that, she decided as they walked under the marquee.

She would make it occupy her entire mind. . . .

"Well?" Matt asked as they emerged from the theater. "Did you enjoy that?"

She had. Very much. But what she'd enjoyed most was his arm around her, his fingers clasped tightly over her shoulder. "I'll probably have nightmares," she said.

His eyes danced as he tilted her face up and looked at her. "I'll go home with you, and stay and protect you if you like."

Dee didn't answer, and they walked the few blocks to her building in silence as the rain hissed down around them.

She knew she'd like it all too well, having him spend the night to protect her, not only against nightmares, but against the deep loneliness that had lived inside her for too long. Just as she could shield him against what she'd seen in his eyes on Thursday night, the fear that she might hate him.

She didn't hate him. She thought there was a strong possibility that she was falling in love with him all over again.

As they stepped off the elevator, he surprised her by saying, "Safe on your front porch, duchess. Thank you for dinner. And for the movie." He'd also surprised her by making no demur when she'd produced prepaid tickets. Before, it had been a point of honor with him that he pay for everything, even after he'd learned about her background. *Especially* after he'd learned about it.

Remembering the way it had been, saying good night to him on her front porch after their first date so many years ago, she linked her hands behind his head, pulled him down, and brushed a kiss over his lips. That's what she'd done so many years before, feeling bold and grown-up. "Good night, Matt."

He set his hands on her waist and pulled her several inches closer. Bending his head, he pressed a kiss to her lips, parting them slightly, sliding the hard, hot tip of his tongue against the narrow seam. "Good night, Dee," he said solemnly, but with a glitter in his eyes, the same one that had been there then. He remembered!

"*That's* how it's done, kid." Word for word. Exactly what he'd told her then.

Reliving that first date, she trembled, no need to act; the same emotions swept over her and quivered through her. She'd moved nearer his warmth then, on a cold

January night, and did so now, in the steamy atmosphere of her solarium.

She tangled her fingers in his hair and drew his head down again. This time her kiss was longer, her mouth a fraction open, moist. The tip of her tongue flicked against his lower lip experimentally. "Like that?" she whispered.

He groaned softly and slid his hands inside her coat, encircling her waist, hooking his thumbs over the links of her belt. "Yeah. Like that. And like this." He touched the point of her jaw with his lips, his breath warm in her ear. "You smell so good," he murmured.

She nestled her face into the crook of his neck and shoulder. "So do you."

With a chuckle he kissed his way down her throat, his tongue seeking, finding, a pulse point, which he tested. "And you taste wonderful."

Greatly daring, she took a tiny nip of his skin. "You too."

"Oh, Lord, Dee!" He tangled one hand in her hair and tipped her face up to his, taking her mouth in a kiss that held nothing back. When he broke it, to lift his head and gaze at her, his eyes were filled with desire, his body hard with it. She moved, a small, surging motion she couldn't help, and he spread his thighs around her, capturing her. Her heart rate went ballistic, and she shuddered, pressing closer to him, her fingers digging into his back.

Step by step, escalation followed escalation as it had

before. He caressed her aching breasts through cashmere and satin until she moaned and arched into him, nipples rigid in his palms. A deep shudder of desire swept through her as a small sound escaped.

"How well I remember this feeling," he said as he slid his hands down over her bottom, curving to mold her buttocks as he drew her ever closer to him, still watching her face. "Do you?"

"Yes!" She gasped involuntarily at the hot, stabbing sensation that surged through her. He stroked her cheek with one thumb. She looked into his eyes. He smiled slowly, and ran the edge of his nail across her bottom lip. She flicked out with her tongue, desperate to taste him, but he withdrew his thumb, stroking it down under her chin. She rose up high on her toes as he brushed his lips over hers, back and forth, resisting the pull of her hands until she cried out in frustration, "Matt, *kiss* me!"

He laughed softly into her hair and cradled her tighter against his arousal. "I didn't then," he said. "Remember? The dragon turned on the porch light. And I was so hard, I could scarcely take a step without groaning, but I left."

She laughed too. "You left. But you came back."

"Hell yes!" He grinned. "And it was like this. . . ."

He showed her how well he remembered, touching her with knowing hands, running his lips down her neck to her collarbone, out to the point of her shoulder. He drew her fingers into his mouth one by one, until she was weak and gasping, yearning for more. "Matt . . .

Matt . . ." she sighed, begging for the kisses, the deep, stirring kisses with which he had wooed her.

"Soon. Wait for it. Feel the need building, Dee. Experience . . . everything with me, the way it was, the way we used to." He took her hand from his nape and drew it around, held it to his throat, against his rapid, hard pulse. "Touch me," he said, as he had instructed her once before. "Learn about what you do to me. Let me know what I do to you. Please, Dee."

She closed her eyes and whispered, "Yes . . ." on a long breath. "Oh, Matt, you make me feel so much! So much that I'd forgotten how to feel."

"That's good." The low, satisfied rumble in her ear was like a reward. "So good, baby . . ."

The scent of earth and tropical blooms hung heavy around them. All was silent but for their breathing, their soft whispers, the sounds of hands against fabric, mouths against skin. His raincoat slid to the floor. Her jacket followed. She opened her eyes and stared at him. She remembered his saying the other night, "You're going to love every last, long minute of it. The way you used to . . ." She was. She did.

He kissed her lids closed. "Accept what's happening between us again, Dee. Enjoy it with me. It won't go any further tonight than you want."

Tonight? But what about other nights? She wouldn't think about that. She'd do as he asked, and accept . . . Enjoy.

The lights were low, the moments precious, as they explored sensation after sensation together. There was a faint jingle as her belt fell to the floor. Then his hands were on her bare back, on her breasts, his mouth drawing her deep, tongue rasping across swollen, hard flesh. Experiencing . . . everything. Again. Reliving the past. Creating the present. Making it sing.

Not considering a future beyond the next caress.

She wasn't sure when the trip down memory lane ended and the present took over, but when she was heavy and trembling in his arms, after what seemed an agonizingly long time, Matt finally covered her mouth with his again. She moaned in pleasure.

He delved deep with his tongue in one powerful stroke that opened her for him, left her reeling. She clung to him, met him thrust for thrust, dug her nails into the skin of his chest between the buttons she'd slipped free. She needed more, more of Matt. The soft, hairless skin of his ribs tempted her, then led her sensitive fingertips on an exploration of the rigid muscles bordering his spine. Her invasion met with impediment, a belt, a waistband, and she tried to slip past it, inside it. Then it was gone, and her palms slipped lower to the elastic of his underwear, which was no impediment.

He groaned and lifted her against him, removing the torture of that touch, sliding her up his body so her legs had nowhere to go, nowhere to cling, but to him. Slowly, he moved her up and down, her skirt riding higher and higher on her thighs, until his hands, under her bottom, were separated from her skin by nothing more than the sheer silk of her underwear.

Dee gasped at the sensation, at the incomparable feel of his chest hairs abrading her nipples, and on the verge of succumbing to the need, felt Matt shudder and hold her very still.

His breath rasped out harshly. "We'd better cool it, babe," he said huskily. He didn't let her go, though, held her as if waiting for her to agree . . . or not.

She knew she wouldn't have to say one word to tell him he was wrong, that cooling it was the last thing she wanted. A movement on her part would have been enough, another kiss, perhaps even so little as a sigh, but a warning tolled somewhere within her. Maybe the same one he had heard. She didn't understand it, but something insisted that she heed it. "You're right," she said reluctantly.

With a deep groan he set her back on her feet and let the fullness of her skirt fall down to cover her again. He pulled her bra together, then drew her sweater down and stood quiet, holding her so tightly, she could scarcely breathe. But she didn't need oxygen to live. She needed only Matt, his arms, his body, his scent.

And the memories. Oh, dear Lord, those powerful, provocative memories their caresses had evoked. That was what the warning had been all about.

Slowly, she pushed the memories back, until she had only the present to deal with. And the uncertain future.

At length he set her from him. She stared at his shirt, the buttons undone, the tail pulled from his trousers. His pants hung half-open. Had she done that, stripped him half-naked? Of course she had. Wanton. Lustful. As only Matt Fiedler could make her. She recalled the feel of the taut, hot skin of his buttocks against her palms.

She flicked her gaze upward, to his face, his hooded eyes. Was he angry with her for taking him up on his offer to stop after going so far? Was he hurt? Disappointed?

He lifted her chin in one large, gentle hand and smiled into her eyes. "Your face is all flushed and glowing," he said. "Your lips are swollen and pink. I love to see you looking that way for me."

She couldn't speak. He traced her damp lips with his thumb again.

"Good night, Dee. My sweet Delight. Dream about me, not about monsters. Okay?"

"Okay." Dee lifted a hand and touched his face. She knew she'd dream about him. Tonight, the next night, and for many, many more.

And then he was gone, leaving a terrible emptiness behind.

In that moment Dee knew she didn't want him to go out of her life again. She wanted . . . him, pride and all.

Forever. She bent and gathered up her chain belt, letting its smooth links trickle across her hand, down her arm. Her entire body was sensitized, ready. Aching.

And Matt was gone.

SEVEN

Surface-cool from her shower, dressed in a silk nightie, Dee lay in her bed staring at the ceiling, thinking about the way it had been, wondering would it be that way again or would it be better? They were both more mature, more able to make reasoned decisions. Was there really a chance for them? Or was her judgment as warped by emotion as it had been with Gavin?

She rolled over and looked at a picture of her father that stood on her dresser. She wished he were there for her to ask. So many times he'd given her the answers to life's most perplexing puzzles and advised her to be strong, to be sure, not to let doubts hold her back.

"If you want something, Dee-Dee," he'd often said, "then go after it. No one can get you the things you want, the things you need, better than you yourself can. Because no one else knows what's right for you."

If he were there, would he have the same kind of unexpressed reservations he'd had when she'd first introduced him to Gavin? As unspoken as those misgivings had been, she had sensed them. She'd seen it in his constrained attitude, and her mother's, toward the man of Dee's choice. But because it *was* her choice, neither had stated the depths of their doubts.

Oh, her mother had said the odd little thing, but always with a smile, as if Gavin's shortcomings were to be seen as charming, though perhaps slightly irritating. Helen would never dream of maligning the man her daughter wanted.

Now Dee wanted Matt. Lord, how much she wanted him! She knew he wanted her too. If she'd invited him in, he'd be in her bed this minute, making love with her. His kisses didn't lie. Nor did his body, leaping to passion each time they moved into each other's arms.

But . . . he had wanted her before, hadn't he?

And he'd walked away.

She looked at her father's faintly smiling image, remembering why Matt had left her thirteen years earlier. Because of who she was. Because, while maybe he was right for her, she was not right for him.

But that was then, she told herself. This is now. Now he has the full confidence of his maturity. This time would he allow her background to drive him off?

She'd failed to recognize his deep feelings of inadequacy when they were in college, hadn't fully realized how her father's position, her mother's seldom-used title, the family wealth, must have intimidated him. She had seen Matt as invincible, and because she hadn't known his vulnerabilities, hadn't understood, she'd made mistakes that had cost them both dearly.

She wouldn't make those mistakes again. But if she made others, would they have such a devastating effect on the man he was now? A man who could not only hold his own in any stratum of society but *knew* he could?

Go after it. No one can get you the things you need better than you yourself can. Her father's words.

And Matt's: *There won't be any seduction, Dee. When you come to me, you'll do it freely, openly, before we so much as kiss*.

It wasn't quite that way. They had kissed. And more. But then he'd broken things off, leaving it to her to decide. If she went to him now, would it be freely, openly, or would she be making a decision based on need for sexual fulfillment?

Yes, passion still ran high through her.

But so did love. And it ran deep.

With a trembling hand she picked up the phone and dialed, then asked for Matt's room. He answered on the first ring, sounding alert, as if he, too, had been lying awake thinking. Or perhaps waiting for a call. Her call.

"I've decided to go to Whistler tomorrow," she said quickly before she could change her mind.

A long moment passed. She listened to the drip of rain

falling on the terrace outside, to the faint crackle of static over the line, to a strange, hollow roaring in her ears.

"Is that an invitation, Dee?"

It was hard to speak with the high, heavy beating of her heart clogging her throat, but she managed to say, "Yes. Do you accept?"

Matt crossed the parquet-floored foyer with Dee and set down their bags. He stared around at this "little" vacation home Dee had bought to enhance her married life.

Her penthouse, with its solarium entrance, gentle blend of contemporary and antique furniture, and its superb location, had spoken of old wealth and supreme comfort with no effort spared to secure it. But it wasn't an especially large place. He hadn't expected it to be. It was, after all, the home of a single woman.

But *this*! This, which she had referred to as a "little place" in Whistler, would have held three of her penthouse and probably half a dozen of the top-notch condo Metcom provided for him in Toronto. She and the man she hadn't married must have planned to entertain a great deal. Or planned a very large family together. His stomach twisted.

The great room, sunk two steps below the entry, stretched away in carpeted luxuriance that Matt could make out only dimly until Dee descended into it to pull open heavy cream linen drapes. Light flooded in through a two-story-high, prow-shaped wall of windows that afforded a spectacular view of the pretty mountain town that spread through the valley below. The cathedral ceiling, sheathed in knotty cedar boards, soared upward to a peak.

Matt followed Dee down into the room before turning in a complete circle. Above the entry, a railed loft stretched the length of one side of the room. Two doors opened from it, suggesting second-floor bedrooms. Opposite that, accessible through patio doors, lay a vast expanse of snow-covered sundecks. They fell away in several levels toward a rushing, ice-embanked stream. On the topmost one, a large, covered hot tub stood, under a deep blanket of snow.

Within, groupings of soft leather furniture with bright, warm-colored cushions on them made cozy conversation areas interspersed with large, leafy plants to break up the space. A baby-grand piano stood in one corner. Surveying it all from a position of honor over the mantel of a massive stone fireplace flanked by bookshelves was a portrait of Dee's father in what must be full ambassadorial regalia.

Matt cringed inwardly at this sharp reminder of the past coupled with the clear and present evidence of the gulf between himself and Dee.

The weight of their financial differences sank onto his shoulders like a cold, wet cloak he had thought he'd finally shed. He'd been wrong. He wished he hadn't come.

He turned another circle and ended facing her. Her eyes were wary, watchful, and her mouth was drawn taut. He managed a short, unconvincing laugh. "So this is what you call a 'little place,' is it?"

She shrugged around the shopping bags she carried clutched to her chest. "All right," she said, "so it's a fair size. That makes a house more . . . versatile, don't you think?"

He had visions of large parties taking place, elegantly clad men and women sipping champagne and nibbling hors d'ouevres after a day on the slopes. People with whom he could never really belong. There'd likely be a cook and a butler in the kitchen for those occasions, and several uniformed maids. If that large family had ever been planned, the children would be tucked away neatly out of sight where they couldn't mess up the professionally decorated perfection of off-white carpets, pearl-gray leather, and solid, honey-colored oak.

Versatile?

Was he versatile enough to overcome the shadows of his past and take the place his education and intelligence had earned for him? With a sick, sinking sensation, he began to suffer serious doubts again.

He remembered the way his parents had entertained: chili and beer. And the way it had been when his aunt and uncle and their five kids had come to spend riotous summer vacations with his family.

"I'll just bet it's versatile," he said, striving for humor

and falling far short. "Think of all the sleeping bags you could throw on the living-room floor when an overload of guests arrive."

Dee winced at the mocking note in his voice. Who was he making fun of, her—or himself?

She looked at his face, saw the dark, brooding expression he wore. This evidence of her financial worth made him feel threatened again. Damn! She wished she hadn't brought him there. She could see that it was happening all over again. It would eat at him, destroy his self-confidence, and if they ever got back together, eventually he'd leave her again.

If he couldn't learn to deal with the reality of her life, there'd be nothing she could do to hold him, any more than there had been thirteen years before.

Her heart broke as she saw the obvious distaste with which he glared at the portrait of her father, his mouth twisted into a pained line.

"Come on," she said briskly, abruptly changing her mind about the possible outcome of this weekend with Matt. They'd ski, and that was all. She'd ski until she was ready to drop. Otherwise, their time together would be unbearable. "Come on." she said again. "I'll show you to your room."

His room? Matt jerked his gaze back to Dee in time to see her turn away. He clenched his jaws with consternation. Had he read this entire invitation wrong?

Obviously.

She marched up the two steps and made to pick up both bags. With a muttered oath he grabbed his and tried for hers. She swung it out of his reach. "This way," she said, leading the way around the wide apron skirting the sunken room to a door that opened, as did several others, directly off it. She handed him the shopping bags containing his new ski clothes and stood back to let him enter.

It was a large, sunny bedroom with a king-sized bed covered in navy and gray. Reflected as it was in mirrored closet doors, the room appeared double in size, and Matt could see an en-suite bathroom through another door to the right of the closet. He was certain all the bedrooms in this house would be so equipped. How many would there be? Five? Six?

Like the great room, this, too, had a stone fireplace, though it was somewhat smaller.

It was a very masculine room, clearly meant for male guests. And just as clearly, she meant for him to stay in it. Alone.

"I trust this will suit you," she said formally. "There are several other guest rooms, so if you don't find this one comfortable, feel free to take your pick of any on this floor."

Ouch! The diplomat's daughter offering hospitality to a less-than-welcome head of an unfriendly state.

He caught her gaze in the mirror. Though she smiled, her eyes held all the warmth of the November sky, and his spirits sank even further. "Why don't you get changed?"

she suggested. "I'll do the same and meet you back down-stairs in ten minutes."

With that she swung away with her own suitcase and disappeared up the stairs, leaving Matt to wonder what in the hell had gone wrong between their alighting from the car, laughing, and her showing him to his room.

Frustration burned like acid inside him. He wanted Dee. Wanted her warm and pliant in his arms as she had been for those wonderful minutes the night before. And he'd convinced himself that her asking him to come with her meant that she wanted him as much. She had been as aroused as he had, Friday evening. It had been visible in her eyes, tangible in the pebble hardness of her nipples, audible in her trembling voice. There had been an echo of that quaver an hour later when she'd phoned to invite him up there. Oh, yes, Dee had wanted him as much as he wanted her.

So what had gone wrong between then and now?

The drive up had been pleasant, with lots of laughter, bright conversation, more good memories popping to the surface with every frothing mountain stream they crossed.

And then it had all changed in the first moments after their arrival.

Matt groaned softly as he sank onto one of the pair of blue suede chairs before the fireplace and toed off his loafers. Yeah, right, those first moments after their arrival—during which he had stood gaping around like a rube, resenting her background, her present circumstances, feeling like a poor country cousin.

He wriggled his toes, then peeled his socks down. Dammit, why hadn't he been mentally and emotionally prepared for the kind of place she'd obviously have in what was well known as one of the most expensive resort communities in the country? Had he thought Dee's being a self-described "shopkeeper" would have brought her down closer to his financial status? Had he believed, on some level he hadn't fully explored, that she was doing something more than merely playing at owning a small chain of boutiques?

Of course not. But social and financial standing shouldn't be an issue between them any longer. He stared at his bare feet, then up at a Robert Bateman of a gray wolf peering alertly, warily, from the shadows in the edge of a forest. He had two Batemans in his own home, and one Remington he particularly prized. Oh, hell, what was he thinking of? Acquisitions weren't important. He was judging himself from the point of view of that reverse snobbery Dee detested.

Disgusted with himself for having acted like a fool, he stood, stripped out of his clothes, hung them in the capacious closet, and dumped out his ski clothes from the bag.

Unfolding a white sweater from his suitcase, he tugged it over his head. He had to hurry. He had to get ready to face her again. And when he did, he would show her that he wouldn't permit the past to conquer either of them. And if it took time to convince her, then he'd spend whatever time was required. But one way or another, he and Dee Farris were going to be together again. Sooner or later, it would happen.

He could only hope for sooner.

Dee shut the door of the master suite. She leaned against it, letting her suitcase thud to the thick pale rose-colored carpet. The room looked exactly the same as when she'd last seen it five years before, with its four-poster tester bed, the canopy the same muted cream, rose, and green floral print as the drapes and spread. It was a room she had decorated to please herself, not the largest in the house by any means, but cozy, intimate, and welcoming.

It was hers.

The house had been meant purely for Gavin. She had chosen it, knowing it was much too large for their needs, because she knew how its ambience would please him. Neither modesty nor moderation were virtues he'd meant to practice once he was married to Dee. He'd so greatly enjoyed the social prestige that her status had brought, and the kind of jet-setting acquaintances—whom he called "friends"—who came almost automatically with her position as her parents' daughter.

To Gavin, the kind of lavish entertaining he'd believed all wealthy people undertook as a matter of course was a thrill. While it would not have been Dee's chosen way of life, she was willing to do it for him.

Gavin . . . He'd delighted in involving himself with the politicians, writers, artists, and other intellectuals he considered his only true equals, and she'd known how proud he'd be, inviting them to a place such as this. His knowing such people, and being on such terms with them that he could casually drop their names into his publisher's column in his magazine, would, he'd been entirely convinced, increase circulation by hundreds of thousands.

Dee crossed the room and swept aside the drapes, looking out onto the balcony where once she had dreamed of enjoying sunrises and breakfasts with Gavin in the summer, and sunsets and kisses leading to long, sensuous nights at any time of year.

While she'd readily recognized his social-climbing bent, it hadn't made her love him less. It was simply his nature. If anything, it had created in her a tenderness for him that verged on pity. She had believed that he'd needed her.

And that was something her only other lover had showed her quite clearly that he had not.

Matt. Her throat tightened.

She sank onto a chair by the patio doors, gazing out at a different view from the one outside the living room. Two such disparate scenes visible from the same house were as much a contradiction as the two dissimilar men who, each in his way, had figured largely in her life.

Here, snowy, forested mountains with icy peaks rising high above the tree line; a massif and a wilderness, looking as if civilization were a thousand miles away. There, a spreading valley where a village fast grew into a town, where lights blazed at night, and its temporary citizens seldom slept. Gavin, she recognized now with the clarity of hindsight, would never have been content with sunsets, sunrises, and her. He'd have been out there among those for whom sleep was a waste of time.

The past—and a man who had coveted her wealth, who would have married her simply to have it. And the present—a man who could never be bought, a man who had once allowed her wealth to drive a wedge between them.

He, of course, was the one she wanted above all.

That terrible look of anguish on Matt's face as he'd gazed at her father's portrait! It was hopeless, yearning for something lasting between them. And without a future for their relationship, could she allow this weekend to take the course she had intended? Would a weekend be enough?

Dee buried her face in her hands. Never.

If only that painting had not been there to remind Matt of all that he had once rejected of her life.

Her mother had given it to her as a housewarming gift.

" A pre-wedding present," she'd said, with a twinkle in her eyes. "For you, not for Gavin."

One of the few occasions when Helen Farris had let slip her less than favorable opinion of Dee's fiancé had come after Gavin complained that the artist hadn't made Dee's father look "handsome" enough.

Perhaps the portrait did play down his better features, but the artist had caught something of his intellectual depth, his strength of character. Dee loved it because it depicted the inner man far more than the polished, urbane image that had been her father's public persona. On that occasion Helen had murmured to Dee that "the lad" was about as "deep as a Dixie cup."

Dee, too, had been hard-pressed not to shake Gavin in frustration after an entire weekend of his obsequiously calling her mother "Lady Helen" every second sentence and agreeing with everything she or her husband said.

About the portrait, her mother had said, "If it comes with the house when you take him there for the first time, what can he say? I wouldn't care to give it to you after the wedding, knowing how he dislikes it; I don't want to be known as 'that kind' of mother-in-law."

As it turned out, she hadn't become any kind of mother-in-law. Instead, she'd become a widow; Dee had learned the truth that her father had uncovered, and she had not become Gavin's bride. She'd been left with serious doubts of her own judgment, doubts that continued to haunt her, as did the memories she wished she could shake.

At length, dressed in her ski clothes, Dee opened her door silently and crossed the loft to look down into the great room. Matt stood facing the windows, hands in his pockets. A stream of sunshine slanted in, burnishing his dark hair. It outlined the shape of his shoulders under his white sweater, cast into relief the narrow, taut hips in dark-colored ski pants. His red jacket lay over the back of a chair, making the room look lived-in for the first time.

And she looked at her father's portrait that seemed to gaze with her, down at Matt.

"A solid kind of fellow," he had called Matt after their single, brief meeting. "He has a good handshake." If her parents had ever guessed at her relationship with him, they'd never let on.

What would Lincoln Farris think of Matt now? Tears ached in her throat. She longed so much for his paternal wisdom; missing him was like a big, open sore that would never fully heal, and returning to this house had torn off the light covering time had put over it.

As if sensing her presence, Matt turned and looked up at her. He smiled.

Dee forced her sadness down deep and descended the stairs.

"This is a beautiful house," said Matt, holding out a

hand for her as Dee came to where he stood. "Thank you for inviting me."

She seemed not to see his hand. "You're welcome." Her tone was polite and level, entirely pleasant, but her eyes were as wary as those of the wolf in the Bateman painting. His conscience raked him with sharp claws of regret for his earlier behavior.

"That's a nice portrait of your father. Who did it?"

Dee's gaze went to the painting. "Margarete Gendron, Vienna."

"Is that where your father was posted after London?"

"Yes." Dee's tone was curt. It was clear she had no wish to discuss her father with him. "Shall we go?" she asked, turning away, but not before Matt saw the shimmer of tears in her eyes.

He caught her hand and pulled her around to face him, tilting up her chin, remembering what she had said about being in this house when the news had come of her father's death. "Dee . . . Is it too painful, being here again? Is it bringing back bad memories?" he asked gently.

Her lower lip jutted out slightly. Her chin had a stubborn tilt as she twisted it out of his fingers. She blinked her eyes quickly as she smiled brightly. "No. I'm fine," she insisted, but he knew she was not. She hung on to her composure only tenuously.

He looked at her for a long moment. "Liar," he said softly, then slid his hand up her arm, over her shoulder, to rest his palm against her neck. Her skin was warm, and he felt her heat soak into him.

Did he feel warm to her? Did his touch please her? Displease her? He searched her face. He wanted to comfort her, to take away the pain he knew must lie like shards of ice around her heart. He'd lost his mother. He knew what it was like. "Why don't we go somewhere else, Dee?" he suggested softly. "There are hotels. Even other resorts. We don't even have to ski. I don't want you to be here if it hurts you."

"No." He watched her swallow, could almost feel the tightness in her throat. There was a certain desperation in her tone as she said, "Matt, let's just go skiing."

For a moment he almost gave in, but then he knew he couldn't leave it like that. He knew her. If she went out onto the slopes like this, tense and unhappy, trying to hide it from him, from herself, she'd end up injured, especially after five years of not skiing.

"We'll go," he assured her. "In a minute," he added, running his other hand under her hair until his fingers linked behind her head. "But first I have to do this."

She didn't resist as he pulled her close, tilted her face up, and bent to brush his lips over hers. "There," he said. "A kiss to make it better."

She stared at the front of his jacket so hard, he began to wonder if he'd left the price tag dangling from the zipper, then she lifted her head and gave him a tentative smile. "I could almost wish you didn't have the knack of reading me so well."

"Did the kiss work?" he asked. "Are you all better?"

She swallowed visibly, then shook her head. "Maybe . . . maybe you'd better try again?"

He laughed softly, delightedly, and pressed another light kiss onto her lips. They pouted beguilingly, and it was all he could do not to plunge right in. But that would have been fulfilling his own needs. Hers were different right now. And hers were paramount.

He smiled at her. She was so beautiful in a red-and-black houndstooth ski jacket and black stretch pants that she could have posed for a ski-lodge ad. Her chestnut hair hung loose around her shoulders, curling lightly. A white hat was tucked under the epaulet on her left shoulder. Gloves protruded from her pockets.

"And another?" he asked. "As my apology for acting like a jerk when we first got here?"

She studied his eyes for what seemed like a very long time, then smiled. "You don't have to apologize. I understood your reaction, Matt."

He nodded. "You always were perceptive, so I'm not surprised that you understood. But I know you didn't like it. Hell, I didn't like it."

"No." Again a shimmer of tears glistened in her eyes. "Matt . . . I can't help what I have. I can't help being who I am."

She wondered if she should tell him about Embassy

Holdings, and her share of it, about the income from it that she never touched because she preferred to live on what she earned herself. But it was there, and like any wealth, it gathered weight even sitting. Before she could form a coherent sentence, Matt spoke. "I know that." He drew a deep breath. "And I can't help some of my . . . reactions."

"Yes. Your pride." Briefly, she brushed the back of her hand across his cheek. "I never wanted to damage that."

At her touch, the sound of her soft voice, a surge of deep desire swept through him. She was so forgiving, so sweet, and her smile so tender, he wanted to crush her to him and tell her all the things he'd never been able to properly say because of youth and inexperience and fear.

She stood on tiptoe and kissed him gently. He hid his flood of emotions with a grin and dropped his hands to her waist. "Was that a kiss to make me better?"

"Yes. Are you . . . okay with things now?"

"I'm not sure," he said lightly. "But maybe another kiss would help."

She gave him one, long and sweet and generous. He welcomed it with a grateful sigh and sudden, urgent trembling he made no attempt to hide. Under his hands, against his body, he could feel some of the tension leaving her. He deepened the kiss, turning it luxurious and sensual, in danger of escalating out of control. They parted and stared at each other.

"One more?" he asked, his breath short. "For . . . uh, give me a minute, and I'll think up a good reason."

A smile hovered on her lips. "Think fast, Fiedler."

He brushed his mouth across hers again. "Okay, but kiss me again while I'm thinking, okay?"

This time their kiss was longer, deeper, more insistent. He tasted her hunger as her tongue met his, mated with it. Her arms linked around his neck. It was hard to resist the longing that hammered through him, the need to sweep her up and carry her to that room she had assigned to him.

Making love would make it better. For both of them. Loving her would be so very, very good. With Dee in his arms he could face anything.

For a moment he tightened his hold on her, then broke off the kiss, and she made a soft, disappointed sound.

"Damn," he said, one hand cradling the side of her face, fingers threading into her hair as he pressed her head to his chest. "I was supposed to be thinking of a reason for that kiss, wasn't I? Know what? I forgot to."

To his delight, his Delight laughed. She leaned back in his arms, and he dropped a series of small kisses over her glowing face.

Quite suddenly, Dee was all better, her blues gone. Her father's portrait seemed to be smiling at the two of them benignly, and with Matt there, the house didn't echo with the shocked, disbelieving cries of her grief. Matt filled it with his presence, as he filled every place he entered, far more effectively than the furnishings she and the decorator had been arranging that terrible day.

"If you can't think of a reason, then I guess I shouldn't kiss you anymore."

"Trouble is," he said, seeking her evasive lips, "when you're kissing me, I can't think."

She laughed again and hugged him tightly. "*Don't* think," she said. She leaned her head back and looked up at him beseechingly. "This weekend, let's neither of us think, or worry about . . . issues, or look anywhere beyond Sunday evening. Let's just ski, and play, and have fun together, as if there's no world outside the boundaries of this village." *And no past. No future.* "Matt? Please?"

He scooped her off her feet and spun her around in a circle. "Yes! Yes! Yes!" he said, kissing her hard and quick for punctuation. "This weekend is ours, Dee. A gift from the gods for the two of us. A slice out of time apart from any other. And when it's over, I promise—"

She cut him off.

"No promises. No words that we might have to take back. Just you and me. The way it once was."

The way it once was! That, he could handle.

"Okay," he said. "You're the boss."

Dee turned her cheek in the curve of his shoulder, rubbing against him like a cat, feeling sheltered and comforted and warmed. His strong arms under her knees and behind her shoulders cradled her easily. And she knew that before this day was out, they'd do much more than ski and play together.

She nearly groaned aloud, aching for what she knew would follow their day of outdoor pleasures. Had she really thought she could get through the weekend and not make love to him? What a notion! It made her want to laugh. It also, foolishly, made her want to cry again from sheer joy. She drew in a tremulous breath, and Matt set her onto her feet again, still holding her close, and stroked his fingers through her hair, searching her eyes.

"Don't Dee. Please don't be sad anymore."

"I'm not. The sun's shining, the powder's deep, and you are here. I'm madly, incredibly happy." Then, with a smile that lifted him higher than the mountain peaks, she backed away and tugged her hat down over her hair.

Matt wished she didn't have to cover even a portion of its glory. "Come on," she said. "Let's go rent you some equipment and hit those slopes."

After a moment, during which he studied her face again, he gave her another very swift, very hard kiss, then opened the door.

She wasn't as happy as she wanted him to believe. Deep inside, the part of her that was a bereaved daughter still ached. Matt knew it. He felt her pain, empathized with it. And he wanted, more than he'd wanted anything for a long time, to erase that grief from her soul, to replace every bit of her sadness with joy.

Together, they ran down the front steps in the cold sting of mountain sunshine, hands linked tightly, like two children escaping from dark and frightening woods.

EIGHT

"That was fabulous!" Dee sprayed snow as she came to a halt, breathless with laughter and exertion, after their first run. Removing her goggles, then her hat, she shook her head wildly. "I'd forgotten how free skiing makes me feel. Like a bird."

He'd forgotten how beautiful the cold air made her skin. It glowed. Her eyes held the blue shimmer of a deep lake in summer. Her hair, loose, whipped by the breeze, fluttered around her face. He grasped two hanks of it and drew it forward, watching the sun pick out red highlights.

"What happened to that awful pigtail hat you had?" he asked, trying to tie her hair under her chin as he had the braids on her hat all those years ago.

She laughed as she pushed his hands away. "It wasn't awful. It was lovely, and completely different from anything I'd ever had before. I adored it. But I think the moths did too," she added as they slid forward into the chair-lift line.

Dee sidestepped to get into position for the lift. Matt followed her, steadying her when she nearly stumbled. "I find I have a lot to relearn after all this time away from the slopes," she said as the chair scooped them up and carried them aloft at a great rate of speed.

"By this evening," he said with a grin, "I'm afraid I'll have muscles that have relearned how to ache in strange ways and places." She, he knew, would hurt even more. He resolved to make her take it easy.

"Don't worry," she said. "You can soak away all the soreness tonight in the hot tub."

He caught her chin in one gloved hand and looked into her eyes. "Will your sore muscles need soaking too?"

The blue of her gaze deepened. Her tongue moistened her lower lip. "Oh, yes," she said. "I'm sure they will."

Matt's heart hammered uncomfortably hard. The mere thought of soaking with her in a hot tub made him ache in far different ways. But it was not an experience he intended to pass up. He didn't intend to pass up anything she offered him this weekend. Even if a weekend was the beginning and end of her offer.

"Who shoveled the snow away?" Matt asked as Dee handed him a large, insulated plastic mug full of hot chocolate. It amused him. He'd never associated anything plastic with Dee. The decks and the pool cover had been cleared as if by elves while they were out on the slopes.

"I have a maintenance service. I called before we left to go skiing and asked to have a few things taken care of," she said.

Yeah. Life could be easy, couldn't it, when all you had to do was call and ask to have things taken care of.

Snatching his mind out of that track, Matt watched Dee walk halfway around the tub to the steps. Steam, made thick and opaque by the submerged lights, rose from the water. It obscured her shape, but memory and imagination tightened his body as she slipped out of her terry-cloth robe and hung it beside his.

He watched her dim, shadowy shape through the mist as she lowered herself into the bubbling water. "Ohh! That feels good!" Her voice came soft and appreciative, reminding him of other times, other circumstances. Times when she had said those same words to him, about what he was doing to her.

Now it wasn't he eliciting her pleasure, but the pulsing jets of water caressing her, the swirling bubbles that burst on her skin as they did on his. He envied them their closeness to her. Would she sigh the same way for him that night?

Her face was a white oval in the darkness as she leaned back at right angles to him and rested her head against a built-in pad. In the soft glow of underwater lighting her body was an indistinct form. Looking straight up, he saw stars blazing brightly overhead. The section of moon they'd seen shining down on the North Shore mountains Monday evening had grown appreciably. A fluttering breeze sent the steam away for a moment, and in the astral glow Matt saw beads of moisture clinging to Dee's piled-up hair, frosting it. Her eyes were closed.

Suddenly, she seemed as remote as the sky, radically different from the laughing woman who had towed him on a tour of the house when they'd returned to get ready for dinner, and had systematically and ceremoniously unplugged every phone there was. "Why are you so far away?" he asked.

She stretched out a leg and touched his shoulder with her foot, drawing the tips of her toes down over his arm to his elbow. "I'm not so far away," she murmured. "Is your chocolate warm enough?"

Belatedly, he took a sip. It was warm enough. The brandy in it went right to his head. Or was it her touch that made him dizzy? "Very warm," he said. "Very . . . sweet."

It would be sweeter if she'd touch him again. He waited, hardly breathing. She didn't touch him again.

But she had. His whole body throbbed in the aftermath of that touch, ached with longing for more.

Dammit, why couldn't he simply reach out and take her hand, pull her closer, see if she was willing? Why did he hesitate with her now when he never had before—not with her, not with any woman he'd really wanted?

He knew. It was because he wanted her more than he'd thought he could possibly want anyone. And it was so much more than sex he needed from her. But if he moved too fast, broke the spell as it was forming, he feared he might lose her.

The thought of losing her again made him sick. What did Dee want? Only this weekend? She had loved him once. He knew that. Could she love him again?

Wasn't that what her invitation had been about? A chance for them to try again? Make that fresh start?

They'd both enjoyed the day despite being out of shape. They'd fallen—together and separately—and laughed, and picked each other up out of the snow and skied again. And he had kissed her in a snowbank.

She'd kissed him back, warmly—no, hotly. Once, on the chair lift, she had kissed him spontaneously out of sheer exuberance.

They'd talked as the day progressed, reminisced, shared with each other bits of their years apart. But nothing deep, nothing important. Only the silly parts, the jokes on themselves, the small, foolish mistakes that keep people from getting too far above themselves, the anecdotes that make up a life. As she'd said that morning, they weren't going to let the outside world intrude.

And they had skied down the hill side by side, the flow of their movements matching, working hard, rushing at a headlong pace, as if eager to finish their last run of the day and get on with . . . something else. They had been so very synchronized, so mated in their movements, that it had seemed even their breathing, their heartbeats, must match.

And their thoughts. Their desires.

He'd thought so at dinner, also. Between courses in the restaurant he'd chosen because it advertised a band, they'd danced, and her body had been soft and warm, almost liquid in his arms, her head heavy on his shoulder. Again, there had been that total communion, a coordination of body language that made him feel as if they were truly one. When he had smiled at her, her eyes had told him things her voice never said.

So there they were, in the steamy, private atmosphere of the hot tub with only the stars for witness . . . and she'd touched him with her toes.

Was it his turn now to make a move?

Languidly, Matt moved his hand through the water. His fingers encountered Dee's ankle and wrapped around it, slid down over her foot. He traced the shape of her instep with the pad of his thumb. She did not pull away.

He eased closer, placing her heel on his thigh, rubbing her toes gently between thumb and forefinger. He felt the shudder that ran through her. An answering one shook him.

He bit back a gasp. This was too fast. He wanted to

make their coming together again a slow, exquisite process, woo her, love her, and . . .

No! Who was he kidding? What he really wanted was to part her legs, thrust fully inside her where she was hot and wet and tight, and . . . and have her. He wanted to take her with all the fury and gusto and fierce need in his body, and none of the finesse he knew she deserved. He wanted that so bad, he could taste it.

But he also wanted Dee to have what was good for her, what would make her moan and writhe and beg and finally climax for him, because that, and only that, would leave him feeling the way he wanted to feel in the end. He wanted more than sex in a hot tub. He was going to *love* the woman Dee Farris had become. After they had gone to bed.

So he slowed himself down.

He slid his fingers up past her ankle to the back of her knee. Removing his hand from her, he picked up his mug and took a deep drink.

Slowly, so slowly that it was a caress, she drew her foot down his thigh and off his knee.

"How are your aches and pains?" she asked, her voice casual, almost belying the throb of tension underlying it. Almost. He smiled. He knew the tension was strung as tightly in her as it was in him, that the heat ran as high.

He fixed his gaze in her direction, though he couldn't make out her features. "My shoulders are a bit tight, but I'll survive. How are yours feeling?"

"My legs were tired, aching before I got in here. But I'm . . . all right now."

For a moment she sipped her hot chocolate in silence, then said so quietly he wasn't sure he'd heard right, "Your shoulders . . . Would a massage help?"

He drew in a harsh breath. If she put her hands on him, there would go any possibility of keeping this a slow and delicious expression of all he felt for her. "Dee . . ." There was a warning mixed with the pleading in his tone, a warning she didn't heed as she slid from where she reclined and came closer to him, water swirling over her shoulders as she stayed deep, out of the cold night air.

"Slide forward," she said, and slipped in behind him. Her hands touched his shoulders, and then her legs floated out around him. He clamped his fingers over her knees in a spasmodic reaction to the brush of her breasts against his back.

He gasped. "You aren't wearing a swimsuit!"

"No," she said, sounding faintly amused. Her legs flexed, and her hand trailed down his spine to meet the edge of his trunks. "But I notice that you are." Her request came, breathless and urgent: "Take it off, Matt. It's going to be in the way. Very, very soon."

He could hardly inhale. He could scarcely speak. But he had to know. He had to be certain. "Lord . . . Dee, are you sure you know what you're doing?"

Her breath puffed warm on the back of his neck, then her lips caressed his shoulders, followed by the nip of her teeth. "What do you think?" she asked. Her fingers and thumbs worked over his shoulder muscles, down his back. "Does this feel as if I know what I'm doing?" She leaned forward to reach his biceps, and her breasts crushed against him. "You used to like my massages."

He groaned as he slid his hands to her ankles, lifted her feet, and crossed her legs in front of him. "I still do." Her massaging hands slid down under his arms, across his chest, her fingers tangling in the hair there, nails scraping lightly over his nipples. He stood it for as long as he could, then pushed off the bench, out into the deepest part of the tub, and let her legs go. As she floated free, he turned and drew her to him, standing with her locked in his arms. Her nipples, hard and pointed, teased the flesh of his chest. Her legs floated up around him again. Her heat pressed to his belly.

Restless hands moved over his back. Her seeking mouth tugged at his earlobe.

"I need to go and get a condom, Dee," he said raggedly. "Stop, now. Oh, love, stop before it's too late!"

She tilted herself back from him, one hand encircling his neck, the other curving around his jaw. "You brought condoms? You were so sure?" she asked. "Of me? Of the outcome of our trip?" He thought she was teasing. It was hard to tell.

Over the loud hammering of his heart he said, "No. I just . . . hoped. And wanted." He clamped his hands under her rump and moved her insinuatingly. "Oh, but I wanted! And still want." He put his hands on her waist and set her back from him. "But I don't want to risk anything that would hurt you, so let me go."

Coming close to him again, she asked, "Do you have anything that would hurt me, Matt?"

"Dee, do you want to get pregnant?" he said on a groan.

"I won't," she said, pressing kisses to his chest, his shoulders, his throat. "That's taken care of." She moved her lower body against him. "Matt, no condom, please, unless you need it for your own peace of mind. You've never been naked inside me. I've never had a—I want you like that."

Never? He wanted that too. Unprotected sex was not something he had practiced since his reckless, uninformed early college days. "Oh, God! Don't . . . do this to me, Dee," he said raggedly as she touched him intimately. "Unless you mean it."

She tilted her head back, and he saw that her eyes were closed, her lips parted, her face dreamy. "I mean it, Matt. I want you. All of you. I've wanted you more and more since the day you came into my store. It's grown too strong for me to ignore. Nothing else matters now. Just you. And me. Together."

Together! Matt exulted at the way her thoughts so closely echoed his. "Yes," he said, and kissed her long and deep. She tasted of chocolate and brandy and Dee. No one had ever tasted quite like her. No one could. "You and me, together," he whispered moments later. "That's the way it should be, Dee." He strained her closer. "It's the way it should always have been."

Her voice was a passionate moan. "I know. I know. Make love to me now, Matt. Here, in the water," she said.

He backed up until a ledge at the far side of the tub caught the backs of his legs, then sank down onto it, drawing her astride his lap. He took the pins from her hair and let its damp curls tumble down over his hands and wrists. Her lips quivered under his, and a sound that could have been a sob shuddered out. He swallowed it as he parted her mouth and claimed her again in a forceful kiss full of graphic intent.

"I've wanted this for so long," he said moments later, cupping her breasts with his hands. "Ah, Dee, you've always been mine."

She drew in a tremulous breath. "I know," she whispered, tightening her legs around Matt's hips. "I want to be yours again. I want you so much I hurt from it. Make me stop hurting."

She raked her hands down his chest to the low band of his bikini trunks, and across the front of them, curving her fingers to mold his shape, moving her hand in the compelling rhythm she'd learned so quickly and so eagerly from him. He murmured his pleasure and lifted his hips in invitation. Twisting off his lap, she tugged his trunks down, and he kicked free of them.

"Come back," he said, feeling bereft without full-body contact. He caught her around the waist and repositioned her. Supporting her shoulders with one hand, he tilted her back in the water and bent to her breasts. He captured a nipple between his lips, then encircled it, his mouth wide as he took in as much of her as he could. "Oh, that feels . . . wonderful," she said.

"Good," he said. "And that?" He sucked the other breast. "Does that feel good, too, my darling?"

"You . . . never called me . . . that before," she said. "You only ever called me kid."

"I thought of you as my darling," he said, lifting his head and blowing gently on her wet flesh. The cool air made her skin pucker. He rubbed his thumbs over the tips of her breasts, making her arch up, begging for his mouth again. "Always, Dee. I was just too inexperienced to say it."

His words thrilled her. "I love to hear it," she said. "I love *being* it."

"My darling. My love . . ."

He whispered more love words to her, all the endearments he had never said before, pressing wet kisses against her wet shoulders and arms and neck. In detail, he told her all the things he wanted to make her feel, all the ways he intended to reach his goal. "Don't tell me," she moaned. "Show me." She tried to stop his words with her mouth.

Laughing, he held back, still talking in a low, sexy voice.

"Matt, stop it," she pleaded. Within, pulses of need throbbed.

He teased her. "Stop what?"

She moved against him. "Oh, you know! You know!"

"How can I know if you don't tell me?" he asked, sounding innocent and confused—and sexy and amused too. "If you don't want me to talk, then you talk to me, Dee. Tell me what you want."

"Oh, you're so cruel," she said on a laugh that cracked at the end. "I want you to . . . do."

"Do what?"

How many times had he done this to her? And how many times had she felt half-wanton, half-embarrassed, and wholly aroused by his demands that she describe her needs in words? She lifted a nipple to his lips. "That," she said.

He kissed her breast, beside her nipple. "That?"

She groaned. "No!"

He kissed the underside of her breast, his slightly bristly cheek brushing over the sensitive, yearning tip. Dee caught his head in both hands and drew his lips to exactly where she wanted them. "Oh, *that*!" he said.

A silly giggle escaped her. It turned into a full laugh as he tilted her back farther, then sang a song for her half-submerged breasts about little white ducks, floating in the water. Then he nibbled them, saying, "Quack, quack, quack."

Matt was such delicious fun in bed—or out of it. "My

governess always taught me that it was impolite to speak with one's mouth full," she said primly.

He laughed and pulled her back up. His words came slightly garbled as he tongued her nipple. "Shall I empty my mouth then? Stop what I'm doing?"

"No." Dee tightened her hands in his hair and drew him even tighter to her. "Don't ever stop what you're doing, Matt. Don't stop." *I love you, I love you!* Had she said it aloud or merely thought it? She didn't know, didn't care. He must feel it, must know it.

She slid closer, clutching his upper arms in her hands, cradling his body between her legs, moving gently against him, glorying in their nakedness, in the feel of his skin against hers, in the warmth of the water contrasting with the cold of the air. Bubbles burst around them, tingling all over, heightening the sensitivity of her nerves. Sexual desire mingled gloriously with tenderness, and love overwhelmed her until it filled her, flowed from her in surging waves.

"Oh, Matt, Matt . . ." She moved spasmodically, need spurring her to frenzied heights. "I want . . . I need . . ."

"Yes, my darling. My Delight. I know. I want, too, and I need." He tightened his hold on her, sucked more deeply while his hand lifted and pulsed around her other breast. Her head spun. Her body craved more.

She took his hand from her breast and moved it down through the water to where she most wanted his caresses.

He slid his fingers over her flesh, parting it, probing, stroking.

"Like this?" he whispered. "Is this what you need?"

"Yes . . ." She moaned, and he slipped two fingers inside her while he worked her sensitive nub. Too soon, deep, hot spasms began within and then flared wildly. "Oh, stop! Matt! It's too much! Too fast."

"No . . . stopping, Dee," he crooned, his face buried against her skin. "Let it happen."

She had no choice. The start of her climax came so suddenly, so irresistibly, that she had no way of controlling it, slowing it, and utterly no wish to. "Matt!" She gasped his name as she lifted, light and buoyant, streaming water. She captured his sex in one hand, held him caressingly, and eased down over him, encasing his flesh in her own.

They both cried out as their bodies joined fully together. She arched her back and shuddered. He was big, hard, as he moved inside her, and she took him deep, needing all of him. "Matt, please!" It was a breathless gasp. "Now!"

"Yes." He clamped the back of her head with his hand, angled her face to his, and took her mouth in an erotic kiss as his fingers continued to stroke over the center of her. His tongue thrust deep in her mouth, his rigid shaft thrust deep into her body, and Dee went frantic, thrashing against him, wanting all that she knew he could give.

She tore her mouth free, flung her head back, and dug her nails into his shoulders. From far away she heard his voice chanting her name over and over, low, harsh, needful. His hips surged, pumping insistently. He drove into her again and again, holding her tightly, hands gripping her thighs, and she rose into the maelstrom of sensations they had created together.

It took a long time for it all to subside.

"Sweetheart?" Matt's voice swam into Dee's consciousness. Aftershocks still pulsed through her. She felt empty without his hardness in her, but fulfilled, too, in a way she hadn't felt for a very long time. Fulfilled emotionally as well as physically. It was such a good feeling, she didn't want to let anything intrude, anything distract her from reveling in it. Water bubbled and rippled around her, caressing her warmly as did Matt's hands. "Are you all right?" he asked.

Her head lolled on his shoulder. She took a deep breath and let it out in a rush. "Mm-hmm."

He chuckled, stroking her hair back from her face. "You hardly seemed to be breathing there for a few minutes."

"I didn't need to."

He kissed her ear. "Why not?"

"Who needs air, when there's you?"

He sighed and ran a hand from her nape to her rump. "Do you know what I need now?"

"What? Whatever it is, if I have it, it's yours."

His laugh came low and husky. "You have it, all right." Deliberately, he ran his hands over her body. "And I'm going to make it mine again. And again. But first of all, I have to get out of this hot water. Maybe you don't know it, but hot tubs make it hard for a man to stay . . . well, hard. I'll do much better in a bed."

She shifted off his lap, and still clinging lightly to his shoulders, raised up several inches, pressed her toes on the edge of the seat he occupied, and flung herself back in an exuberant splash, all arms and legs and kicking feet.

Matt held up his arms to keep the water out of his face. "Impossible," Dee said, surfacing at the far side of the big oval tub and stepping out, a sleek silver form in the mist.

"What's impossible?" Matt shivered as the cold air wrapped around him.

She tossed his robe to him, then whipped hers across her shoulders and shoved her arms through the sleeves. His robe was as cold as the air, and slightly stiff with frost. It melted on his body when she stepped right up to him and slid her arms around his waist inside the cloth. "You, doing any better than that."

"Wanna bet?" he asked as he lifted her off her feet.

"Yes. I'll risk a wager," she said. He carried her across the deck and into the warmth of the house. The fire still glowed faintly on the hearth.

He sat her on a large, soft ottoman between an easy chair and the fireplace, then added another couple of logs.

The flames licked at them greedily. "What are the stakes?" she asked.

He chuckled and parted the front of her robe, baring her body to the flickering light of the fire, and to his hands, his eyes. He kissed one nipple, his tongue a greedy flame on her skin. "I win, I get to make love to you twice before breakfast."

She slid her hands through his hair, holding his head to her breasts. "And if I win?"

"You get to make love to me three times before breakfast." He sucked a nipple deep into his mouth, pressing it with his tongue.

"What time is it now?" she whispered after several moments has passed.

"Mmm, I'd say somewhere between darkness and dawn. Nowhere near breakfast yet. We have hours in which to conclude our wager."

"Oh. That's . . . good."

His lips trailed down her stomach. He clasped her under the arms and laid her back on the ottoman so that her head and shoulders rested on the seat of the chair behind. Moving between her knees, he pressed kisses over her abdomen, dipped his tongue into her navel.

"Matt . . . I thought you said you wanted to go to bed." He felt her legs trembling against his shoulders.

"I do. But I want this . . . more. And first."

He parted the soft, wet curls between her legs, stroked

his tongue over her, and Dee knew she wanted that more too. More than anything.

Tenderly, sweetly, he took her to a shattering climax, then gathered her damp body into his arms, lying on the thick carpet with her, content now simply to hold her.

Dee sighed, a long, tremulous sound of total satisfaction. Matt rose up and filched a couple of cushions from the nearest sofa. Tucking one under her head, the other under his shoulder, he leaned over her, wrapping her robe warmly about her. "Regrets, my darling?"

She smiled and traced his face with a languorous fingertip. "No. You?"

Slowly, he nodded. "Just one."

Her eyes widened as she half sat up. "What?"

"That I didn't get a chance to see your sexy lingerie and take as long as I wanted getting you out of it."

Dee laughed and flopped back down. "There's always tomorrow," she said.

"Is that a promise?"

For a moment she didn't answer. Then she said, very solemnly, very carefully, "Yes, Matt. Tomorrow. That's a promise."

Matt drew her head against his shoulder and lay stroking her body until the coals in the fireplace were gone. She'd promised him tomorrow. He'd pretend that was enough.

Presently, they arose and went up the stairs to her room.

As she turned on one bedside lamp, Dee saw Matt's gaze take in the big four-poster bed, the sofa and chair in the sitting alcove, a small table with two comfortable dining chairs pushed under it, near a window. His jaw clenched. She knew what he was seeing. And hating.

Sliding her arms around him, she smiled into his brooding eyes. "This is the first night I've ever spent in this house, Matt. I can't begin to tell you how glad I am to be spending it with you."

A hint of shame showed in his eyes at being caught, but he smiled through it. "You're a witch, you know. It should scare the hell out of me, how well you read my moods."

She laughed. "If I let myself get frightened each time you picked up on one of mine, I'd never cease running."

Filling his hands with her hair, he kissed her with tenderness that brought tears to her eyes. He kissed them, too, and lay back on the bed, carrying her with him. "What would you say if I told you I'd quit running, Dee?" He pressed his face to her heart. "That I think I've found my home. Right here in you."

She didn't reply. Not in words. But Matt thought her response was more than adequate.

"Who won the bet?" he asked, when he had breath with which to speak.

She stroked her fingers over his hairy chest. "Does it matter?" With the down comforter pulled up around them, she snuggled close to his side. "I'm not sure I even recall what it was."

He smiled. "No, it doesn't matter. I think we both won, don't you?" Then, rolling away from her, he shut off the light.

"I know we did."

"Dee . . ." She felt the bed shift slightly as he moved. From out of the intense dark his voice was low, disembodied. "I have to say this. I wasn't going to. But—I love you. I don't know if it's still, or if it's again. I only know I'm in love with you. Do you . . . mind?"

Mind? She squeezed her eyes tight shut. "I love you too, Matt." Hadn't he heard her saying the words over and over while their bodies were joined? Or had she said them only silently?

His "Good" was nothing more than a soft whisper, like his kiss as it brushed her lips.

"Sleep now, my darling," he said several moments later, and rolled away.

Dee reached toward him, felt nothing but the bed with the arc of her sweeping hand, heard nothing, not even his breathing. Suddenly, the darkness, the loss of his touch, sent an almost surrealistic apprehension through her, an awful feeling of sensual deprivation.

"Matt! Where are you?" At her cry his hand came out and caught hers. She clung to it, to him. "Stay with me," she begged, wrapping him tightly in her arms, flinging a leg over his hip.

"I'm here. I'm not going anywhere," he said, holding her with fierce strength and promise. "I moved away because before, you never liked to spend the night in my arms. You wanted your side of the bed to yourself."

That was true, she had. Then she had needed space. But now . . . "I want you on my side of the bed tonight," she said, and was astonished at the tremor of fear she heard in her own voice. But no force of will could contain it. *Tonight, and every night.*

Stop it, stop it, she told herself. This is Matt. This isn't . . . Yet maybe because it was Matt, the fear grew more intense. Like the love she felt for him, it overwhelmed her. "I need you, Matt!" she cried, clinging tightly. "I need you so much! Don't leave me. Don't leave me again." She pressed herself to him as if by this very closeness she would ease the terrors of being alone.

Their having found each other had been pure serendipity, but there was no guarantee that this time they'd have any better chance than when they were in college. But she wanted it so terribly, a future with Matt.

"Sweetheart, relax," he said, sliding long, soothing strokes down her back and up again to her nape. "I'll stay with you, love, for as long as you want me."

Forever, Dee said, but not aloud. He had promised her that once before and reneged. Nor had he been the only one.

This time full trust and belief would come harder.

NINE

"Hey, don't go away," Matt said, tumbling Dee down onto the bed beside him. "Don't I see two cups on that tray?"

She rested her head on his shoulder while he slid a hand sensuously over her satin-clad hip, slowly sliding her knee-length robe upward. "I wasn't going far," she said. "Only back to my side of the bed."

"Yeah. That reminds me." He pushed her erect and looked at her through narrowed eyes. "Your side of the bed. What was that all about last night, Dee?"

Her face grew haughty. "I don't know what you're talking about."

"No?" He lifted her over him, piled pillows behind her, pulled the duvet up under her arms, and passed her her coffee. Shoulder to shoulder, hip to hip, they sipped.

"I think you know perfectly well what I'm talking about," he said presently.

She shrugged and took another sip of coffee, flicking him a glance from behind her tumbled bangs. "People change in thirteen years. When I first started sleeping with you, I had never shared a bed with anyone. It takes some getting used to."

He nodded. "So you got used to sleeping with someone, finally. It wasn't me." She had never wanted him to cuddle her while she slept. It rankled like hell, thinking she had learned that pleasure from some other man. He knew he should leave it alone, but he couldn't. "Who, Dee? Your fiancé?"

"Yes." She said only the one word, and in a tone that left him in no doubt about her lack of intention to say more.

Silence fell, tense and uncomfortable.

Matt turned his head and looked at Dee. Her eyes were closed as she leaned back on the pillows and drank her coffee. As if sensing his stare, she opened one eye and glanced at him quickly before closing it again. Then, gently, almost absently, she began sliding the arch of her foot up and down his calf, the hem of her short robe brushing over his genitals.

He stood it for perhaps three minutes, then took her cup from her, set it on the tray, placed his own beside it, and slid down in the bed, carrying her with him.

She clung to him. "I don't want to think of anything

but how good it was to wake up with you beside me, Matt. Touching me. Holding me. I thought I'd never—" She broke off to press small, hot kisses on his neck and shoulder, nips on his chest. In one more minute he'd lose control of things, but he hated unfinished sentences, unfinished business. And Dee, he thought, had something eating away at her, inside.

With her head nestled back on his shoulder, his arms holding her close, he said, "Tell me about it, Dee. What happened to leave you so scared of being alone in the night?"

For a moment she didn't respond beyond going rigid in his arms. "I am not scared of being alone in the night. Really, Matt, you make me sound like a child, afraid of the dark."

"Last night you were afraid when I rolled away from you."

She slid away from him now, propped herself on an elbow, and stared through a tangle of hair. The duchess debauched. He wanted to smile. He did not.

"You're clearly mistaking passion for fear," Dee said, wishing she had maintained better control the previous night. Matt was not Gavin. Matt was not about to leave her bed and slip out in the night to . . . "I love you. Is it so strange that I wanted to be close to you?"

"I 'clearly' know the sound of an upset woman when I hear her cry out to me in the dark," he said. "You thought I was gone."

She shrugged and conceded the point. "A precedent has been set, counselor."

"Balls." Matt wasn't going to be swayed. "Last night's panic attack had nothing to do with my having left you before. It was believing I'd left your bed that disturbed you. And I would like to know why."

His eyes narrowed as he zeroed in on that which she least wanted to share. "Tell me about your engagement, Dee. That was a very important part of your life, and I know nothing about it."

Dee clenched her teeth. "You know all you need to know. It existed. It ceased to exist. I never discussed you with Gavin, Matt. If you expect me to discuss him with you, then I'm afraid you'll have to be disappointed."

She slid out of bed on her own side and headed for the sanctuary of her dressing room and the bathroom beyond. As she rounded the foot of the bed, Matt lunged, caught the back of her robe, and tried to hold her back. She shrugged out of it and let it fall, hearing his laugh behind her.

Before he could do anything further to delay her, she slammed the door hard.

"I'll have to be disappointed, will I?" Matt muttered, and flung open the door. Through the next one, also firmly closed, he heard the shower come on in the bathroom. "Have I got news for you, duchess." He grinned as he stared at the door and thought about Dee's pretty, sleek, and very bare backside as she'd marched away from him. And about her short satin robe that he held in his hand. There was also the terry one she'd left in the living room. Unless she had some garment that he hadn't noticed in that pristine bathroom of hers, she'd come out of there wrapped in a towel, intending to armor herself with clothing in the dressing room before seeing him again.

He grinned as he opened closets, which, for the most part, were empty. He had news for her on that issue too.

Before the shower stopped, Matt had poured himself another coffee, climbed back into bed, and reclined on a comfortable stack of pillows. Right on schedule, Dee came stomping out of her dressing room, wrapped in a large blue towel, her hair secured under a smaller one. He had never actually seen someone in bare feet stomp. Her eyes glittered like bits of the frozen sky.

"Where is my clothing?"

He grinned. "Why would you want clothing, duchess? I had plans of keeping you naked and out of breath for the rest of the morning."

"Matt, this is not funny!"

He chuckled and patted the bed invitingly. "I see a certain amount of humor in it." From under the pillows he extracted a filmy garment. "But if you insist. Here's something. If you'd like to put it on, I'd love to watch you do it. Before we talk."

It was nothing more than a very sheer teddy in ecru silk tricot, with delicate insets of cream-colored lace. She'd packed it thinking how Matt would enjoy taking her out of it. It had never occurred to her that he might want to watch her put it on. Donning such a garment was never quite as elegant or as graceful as removing it, and even with it on, she'd in no way feel dressed enough to cope with the confrontation she knew he intended to force.

Obviously, Matt, like Gavin, well understood the power of clothing, and how vulnerable an unclothed person could feel. She was surprised he wasn't dressed in a three-piece suit and a power tie, the better to intimidate her.

He flipped back the covers and swung his legs off the bed, completely naked himself, and Dee felt ashamed of the thoughts that had winged across her mind. Of course this wasn't about power. Matt sought his sources of power in other ways.

He held out the teddy again.

"Thank you," she said, reaching for it, meaning to snatch it and run. He was too fast for her. He caught her wrist in a gentle manacle of strong fingers and tugged her right up to the side of the bed, between his knees.

He hooked his other hand in the towel twisted together over her breasts. His fingers were warm and hard against her skin, reminding her of what his touch could do to her. Her nipples peaked in response.

His gaze, fixed on hers, was full of love, caring, compassion. "Did you really think I'd let you run away, Dee?"

"Matt . . ." She wanted, very badly, to argue,

though she'd already concluded while in the shower that he had as much right to know about that part of her life as she had to know about his past history. She shook her head, dislodging the smaller towel. It lay cool and damp on her shoulder before sliding to the floor. "It's simply a period I don't like to think about, let alone talk about. I came out of that engagement with my self-esteem in tatters, feeling like a fool."

She forced herself to go on looking at him. "Feeling . . . ashamed. And hurt. And . . . guilty, because I should have sensed what was happening." Her voice cracked, but she went on. "But I didn't. I believed Gavin loved me for myself. I couldn't see any reason why he wouldn't. So I let my ego, as well as my libido, cloud my judgment.

He searched her face, a faint frown between his brows. "That's not unusual, Dee. It happens to everyone. There should be no guilt in it, love. No shame. Hell, there've been times, especially in the past six days, that my libido hasn't just clouded my judgment, it's buried it under an avalanche."

On the last word Matt dropped his hand, carrying her towel with it. Then he wrapped his arms around her and lay back. "And I don't see any reason, either, why your fiancé shouldn't have loved you as much as you believed he did."

She lay atop him, startled by the sudden change in position and comforted by the expanse of warm skin pressed intimately to her body. It wouldn't have been the same, had Matt let her retain her towel. She laid her head on his chest, sliding her arms around him, holding tight. "Yes," she said, "but as you said, maybe your judgment's not what it should be right now."

"I'm not worried about it," he said, stroking her back with long, soothing motions of both hands. "Tell me, baby. Tell me what went wrong."

Dee sighed and nodded. Yes. Now she could tell Matt.

Somehow, without letting her go, he managed to twist them both around until they lay in the bed with the eiderdown pulled over them again. Dee's head, damp and sweet-smelling, rested on his shoulder. He stroked her hair. And waited.

"I met Gavin at a party. He was ten years older than I was, handsome, charming, knowledgeable, and we hit it off immediately. He offered me a job on the weekly news magazine he published. I grabbed the chance. When he mentioned a week or two later that because he lacked the funds to swing it, he'd just turned down an opportunity to buy the magazine, I was happy to provide investment capital.

"At first he said he didn't want me to do that, that I should look after whatever 'little nest egg' I had. In order to convince him, I told him about my family, and he acted so amazed that I truly believed he'd had no idea who I was. I found out later I was wrong. He acted . . . devastated, too, and when I insisted he tell me why, he said that he'd fallen in love with me the night we met, and had offered me a job so he could be near me. He'd been about to propose marriage, he said, but now that he knew, of course he couldn't."

She lifted her head and met Matt's gaze for a moment. "It wasn't an attitude that surprised me, somehow."

Matt nodded. He could see the parallel himself. "Go on."

"I persuaded him to take my money; hindsight tells me that he let me persuade him. I argued that once he was in a position to direct policy, we'd be better able to place the focus where we both wanted it. Our main thrusts were ecology and the economy, and how they impact on each other, how, for the good of all, a proper balance must be struck and maintained. I honestly believed, still believe, that we were making a difference, and was glad of a chance to make more of one."

She caught Matt's hand and held it tightly. "I felt really good about having to persuade him," she added with a small, bitter laugh, "and even better when he listened to me with respect for my ideas. I told him that once the magazine was up and running the way we both intended it to, if he insisted, he could pay me back the amount I'd invested. He promised, most fervently, that he would. I believed him because I believed *in* him.

"I also trusted in his love. After all, hadn't he fallen for me when he thought I was another unemployed journalist looking for work?" She didn't say, *The way you fell for me when you thought I was an ordinary freshman at McGill*, but Matt heard the echo of the words nonetheless.

"So he let me convince him that we should marry," Dee went on. "I thought my future was all mapped out, and although I sensed that my parents didn't care much for Gavin, I was of age, and they never tried to influence my decision. Then, a few days before the wedding, I was in this house overseeing the placement of the last few pieces of furniture. I planned the whole place as a surprise for Gavin. I was bringing him here for our honeymoon. He'd left all those arrangements to me."

Dee felt Matt's arm stiffen under her and closed her eyes, waiting for a scathing comment. Matt, of course, would never have let his wife-to-be not only plan the honeymoon but pay for it, or buy a house for him. The expected outburst didn't come.

"As I told you before, I was here, and a call came for me to go to my mother." Her voice went high and thready. "My father was . . . gone." Matt's embrace tightened, and Dee steadied herself within it, found strength because of it.

"Just like that," she said. "No warning, no nothing. He'd been at his desk in the library in their home in Victoria, going through some papers, and Mom was sitting nearby, reading. They often did that, sat together though Dad was working. He'd retired from the diplomatic service but still ran the family business, Embassy

Holdings, out of his house. She heard him make a sound, looked up, and he was falling from his chair."

She was glad Matt only held her a little tighter. She hated it when people murmured things like, "At least it was quick." Or, "He didn't suffer." He *had* suffered. On her behalf. And for a long time she had lived with the guilt of thinking that maybe that pain, that shock, had killed him.

She went on, her voice small and shaky again. "When I was clearing off his desk so the lawyer could use it for the reading of the will, I saw exactly what he'd been checking over at the moment of his death. It was a report on Gavin. From a detective agency. It detailed Gavin's life for the past fifteen years, through two marriages he'd neglected to mention, four children he was failing to support, and several affairs, all with wealthy women."

She cleared her throat and went on, a thread of anger giving her voice strength. "He was having an affair even then, while I was dreaming about our future, decorating the homes we'd share, planning our honeymoon.

"Over the months of our engagement I'd begged him to move in with me, or let me move in with him. He'd always said that if I was less precious to him, he'd agree. But he valued my reputation, my family name, and respected my parents far too much to risk behavior they would surely find reprehensible.

"But . . . that didn't mean he didn't want to sleep with me. Or, at least, have sex with me, yet he never once spent a night in my bed. And whenever he left me, according to the detective's report, he went to his other woman. From my bed to hers. She lived only two blocks away. He had moved her there for his convenience."

"Dee . . ." Matt's voice rumbled. "You don't have to—"

"Yes, I do." She rose up, hauling the comforter with her, and sat looking down at Matt. "I asked if he loved her. He said no. It was just that sex with her was sensational. His word, not mine. I was for class, power, and status. And money, of course, but he didn't come right out and use the word. Maybe, to him, the other words he used equated money. But she was for fun and pleasure. He didn't expect a woman of my 'breeding' to be good in bed. It wasn't required."

Lines of tension radiated from her eyes, around her mouth. Matt wished he'd never asked to hear this story. He wished she would stop, but he knew that now she needed to tell it right to the end.

"He truly didn't understand why he couldn't have us both," she said, and even now sounded and looked as perplexed as she must have been then when first faced with Gavin's amorality. "He promised, when he knew he'd been caught, to keep his relationship with her as discreet as it had been all along. He said that I'd never miss out on anything. He'd make love to me any time I wanted. He'd give me children.

"Children! He thought I'd still want his children! He

had no comprehension of the need for trust, faith, fealty in marriage, all the things necessary before I'd have conceived a child.

"He had no intention of giving up his lover. He'd wanted her enough to lie and cheat before the wedding, and plan a whole lifetime of fraudulence afterward, simply so he could have her. He thought he could have us both, *should* have." Again that baffled expression crossed her face. A small laugh escaped her.

"Some kind of twisted logic told him he deserved everything he wanted, simply because he wanted it. She gave him the good sex, but I gave him the social position he had decided was his right. He felt my presence by his side gave him more clout, made him more believable to the people he wanted to cultivate. He never failed to drop the information that my maternal grandfather was the earl of Monmount. And I . . ."

Dee shook her head. "I was too stupid to see it. It took my father to make the inquiries that I should have made myself. And he died knowing he'd have to show me what he'd uncovered, and knowing he would have to hurt me unbearably in doing so.

"My dad . . ." She smiled now. "He liked you, Matt. He told me so that summer when you and I were first apart. He asked if I'd be seeing you again." Her smile faltered as she added, "I told him I would. He was pleased." Her smile strengthened again. "He said you had a good handshake."

Matt felt as if someone had just pinned a medal on him. He rubbed a hand over his bare chest. "Thank you for telling me that. It"—He cleared his throat—"means a lot." He hitched himself up to sit beside her, pushing her wildly curled hair back from her cheek. It was mostly dry now.

"You persuaded yourself that thinking about having to give you the results of his investigation was what killed him, right?"

Dee nodded. "I know now that was an overreaction, but for a long time I had difficulty with it."

"I can understand that. I thought for quite a while that if my mother hadn't had to work so hard after I cost her about ten years' savings, she never would have gotten cancer."

They shared a smile. It was good, Matt thought, to have been able to tell her he understood, and to know that she knew he did.

It was good that they could share.

He linked his hands behind her head and pulled her face close to his. "Know what?" he said.

"No, what?" They smiled about that too.

"If you had brought that son of a bitch here for a honeymoon, even for a weekend, for so much as a minute, I'd trash this house with the first baseball bat I could get my hands on so you'd never have to picture him in it."

Dee blinked against the sudden stinging in her eyes.

"Good thing I didn't then. I don't own a baseball bat. You'd have had to make do with a tennis racket."

"I don't know how to play tennis."

"I'll teach you," she offered.

"Nah," he said, gliding one hand up under a breast, fingering the nipple. "I'd feel silly in a little white outfit. Bad enough I had to learn to play golf so I could entertain Edwin's business contacts with him. I wear the shoes and the glove, but I don't wear the stupid hat."

"Tennis is quite macho, and you wouldn't have to wear anything you don't like."

He gave her a wary look. "You like tennis, huh?"

She nodded.

"All right. I'll learn. But no white suit."

She nodded again. "And will you teach me how to play baseball?"

"Sure," he said with a lascivious grin. "I do my best work with a club."

Dee rose, straddled his body, and lowered herself to his lap. "Tell me about it," she whispered.

"Let me show you instead."

Matt and Dee ran laughing through the rain, hand in hand, from her car to the main terminal building. They stopped, breathless, at the check-in counter, and Dee gasped out her name as Matt set her bag on the scales. "My secretary arranged to have my tickets waiting here for me," she said. "Sorry I'm late for check-in."

"Oh, yes, Ms. Farris." The man gave her disheveled appearance a sweeping look. He wasn't accustomed to first-class passengers arriving in such a state. She swallowed another laugh, thinking of what he'd think of the contents of her weekend bag. One tracksuit and half a dozen frothy items, well pawed by a pair of large hands. But there had been no time to go home and pack.

The man scribbled something on a paper, spoke briefly into a phone, and said, "We'll have to hurry. If you'll come this way, please, we can expedite your clearance and . . ."

Whatever else he said, Dee missed. Matt held her tightly, as tightly as she held him. "A week," she murmured. "I'll call you when I get to Toronto next Monday."

"Call me before that. Call me at my hotel, tonight, to let me know you landed safely. Call me tomorrow, before you get out of bed, to let me know you still love me. Call me anytime, Dee. Call me every time you think of me."

She clung more tightly. "I don't know if they'll let me keep a transatlantic line open twenty-four hours a day. Oh, Matt, I don't want to go!"

"I know." His kiss was hard and possessive, his arms two compelling bands that tried to press her body into his. "I don't want you to go. But you'll be back, Dee." He cupped her head in his hands, tilted her face up. "And I will be waiting."

She searched his eyes for a long moment, reading

there the solemn promise he made, the truth of it, and knew that from this time forward, he would never break his promises again. Her kiss was hot and wet and desperate in its need. Matt met that need, tried to fulfill it, but it built his own craving so remorselessly, he had to break it.

She blinked at him. "Whew!"

He nodded. "'Whew!' just about covers it for me too." He swallowed hard. "Now go," he said, grinning. "That poor little fellow dancing over there behind the counter is about to pee in his pants from anxiety."

Dee left him, laughing.

Her laughter died as Dee matched her stride to that of the airline employee who guided her toward the gate. As they approached the swinging doors that would cut her off from Matt, she turned for one last look and saw his fawn raincoat flapping at the backs of his knees as he strode toward the exit. His head up, his broad shoulders back, his long legs purposeful, he did not turn.

A sense of wrongness flooded Dee as she went through a different set of doors. No! She and Matt should not be heading in opposite directions. They must not. Her breath caught, held. She swallowed. And stopped.

"I'm not going."

The man caught her arm. "But your bag—"

"What does it matter? The clothes in it are all wrong for Paris anyway."

"You're not going because you packed the wrong—"

Dee laughed. "No. Yes. I—I must go. Now." She

twitched her elbow from his grasp, turned, and ran after Matt. A tour group interposed itself in her path. She fought her way through the crush, but by the time she had cleared them, Matt had long since disappeared through the exit. Dee ran faster, thrust her way outside into the lashing wind and rain, where low-hanging clouds held back the approach of daylight. Matt was gone.

No. Not yet, he wasn't. She saw her car rolling toward the exit, stood, and watched him go, the rain beating on her bare head, soaking her. A commissionnaire deferentially touched her arm. "Miss? Do you need a taxi?"

"Yes," she said. "A taxi is just what I need. Though I suppose it's too late to tell the driver to follow that car."

It was, Matt thought, going to be one hell of a long week. As he parked in his hotel's parking garage, he relived Dee's last kiss. Its warmth and sweetness lingered in his heart like a song. It hadn't been a kiss of good-bye, but one that said, "Remember me," one that said, "There's more to come."

Oh, yes. To be sure. There was much, much more to come for him and Dee.

In his room he flopped on his bed. It was an hour or more before he'd have to meet Edwin and the others for breakfast as was their custom. He glanced at the phone where a red light flashed, but he flipped a sheaf of papers over it. Messages could wait. They'd likely been waiting all weekend, and with the Chang deal concluded, they couldn't be terribly important.

Now he wanted simply to lie there and think, to remember, to relive each precious moment of the weekend past. The entire week! Had it been only one week ago that, as a key player on the Metcom team, he'd walked into the Westmarch Apartment Hotel and seen a store called Sheer Delight?

Metcom. His job and Dee.

He could not have both. That much was obvious. Their living a whole continent apart simply wouldn't work. He closed his eyes, seeing the way it would be, him and Dee, together. He envisioned her penthouse, the solarium, the red macaw. He saw her boutique, smelled the erotic, exotic scent of it. He tasted it on Dee's skin.

Someone called him, wanting to drag him away from Dee. He resisted the call, then heard it again. "Matt. Do it. Do it now." He looked up, and it was Edwin, a dim and shadowy figure standing on the far side of a gutted building.

The walls were patchy, stripped of everything; bare, dead wires hung loose; glassless windows gaped. Gone was the antique furniture, the warm, moist solarium where he had nearly lost his mind and taken Dee on the hard floor while tropical birds muttered their disapproval. He saw dynamite charges set inside the shell of the beautifully constructed old building, condemned, not because it had failed in its purpose, but because it was in the way of someone else's purpose.

A large part of him rebelled as he saw the demolitions expert key the button. No, not some nebulous figure, not some strange hand; it was his own. The realization came as a shock. His breathing labored, he tried to stop his finger from reaching out, tried to recall the muscular impulse sent by his brain. But the synapses had closed, the command had been issued for tendons to pull, muscles to flex, finger to push. He wanted, terribly, for this not to be happening. But his brain ordered; his body obeyed. His flesh pressed against hard plastic and, sweating, gasping for breath, he watched as, in awful silence, the granite blocks collapsed in on themselves, turning to rubble even as they fell.

And there, in the rising dust, delicate lingerie lay scattered, bits fluttering in the gales of the explosion. And with them Dee's face, her hands reaching out to him from the ruins of her home. And then, like a memory, she went floating away in a gray cloud, while bright red and yellow feathers fluttered down.

"No!" The sound of his voice woke him as he sat up, recoiling from the nightmare. "Oh, God . . ." He groaned, rubbed his face, then peered at his watch. His hour was gone. The breakfast meeting was due to start in ten minutes. Though, technically, he might not be expected to attend, he wanted to know how the final signing had gone.

Besides, it would take his mind off Dee's departure. Holy hell, what a dream that had been!

He flung himself off the bed and dived for the shower. Standing under the spray, he remembered the showers he and Dee had shared. The week loomed unbearably long. He would have liked to spend the day alone, immersed in thoughts of Dee, but there were other deals pending, other people to see. Since he hadn't gone home, Edwin would expect him to be on duty.

The phone shrilled as he stepped out of the shower. Rubbing a towel over his head, he picked up the receiver.

Problems, he thought as he finished drying himself, frowning over the brusque tone of Edwin's demand that he present himself at once. "Problems," he said with a laugh as he rode up in the elevator to his boss's suite six floors above. Edwin tended to panic at the closure of every deal. He frowned.

But that deal had been closed on Friday, hadn't it, and nothing else was anywhere near completion. What kind of problem could have arisen since Friday? Whatever it was, he hoped it was one he could sort out quickly.

He had a date in Toronto next Monday night, and no matter what, it was one he meant to keep.

TEN

Dee alighted from her taxi and stared at the marching crowd outside her building. Elderly ladies in plastic rain bonnets marched beside men with long hair and unkempt beards. Old men with erect bearing carried signs as proudly as they'd once shouldered rifles to protect their country.

SAVE THE WESTMARCH, a placard read. And DON'T LET THE WESTMARCH DIE. EASTERN RAPISTS GO HOME. MY BABY DESERVES A HERITAGE. SAVE A NEIGHBORHOOD—BULLDOZE METCOM. CITY HALL—JUST SAY NO!

Dee did a double take. *Metcom?*

She forced her way through the packed picketers and up the steps under the canopy. "Jenkins! What is this?"

His seamed face was worried. "I'm not certain, Miss Farris, but it appears that the building has been sold. To a company called Metcom. Those people say the new owners mean to demolish us. It can't be true, can it, Miss Farris? Would the city allow such a thing?"

Dee's face felt frozen as she listened to Jenkins. "No," she said. Her voice sounded cold even to her own ears. Cold and frightened. "Matt," she whispered, looking out over the crowd. "Metcom? Matt? Demolish the Westmarch? No. Matt loves old buildings."

She swayed, and Jenkins steadied her, led her toward her elevator, keyed it open for her, and ushered her in. "Are you all right, Miss Farris? Shall I call someone?"

Dee shook her head. "No. No, thank you, Jenkins. I'll be . . . fine. I'll call . . . someone." But as the elevator doors shut, she leaned her head back against the dark paneled rear wall and moaned softly. "No," she said. "Oh, Matt . . . Please, no . . ."

In her apartment she dropped her purse on a table and went right through to her bedroom. She lifted the phone, noticing how her hand shook, glanced at the number she had scribbled on a notepad Friday night, and punched it in.

"I'm sorry. Mr. Fiedler doesn't answer. Would you like to leave a message?"

Dee hung up and punched in a memory code. "Mom! Oh, thank goodness. I've got a big problem. Someone's bought the West—"

"Don't worry, darling," Helen interrupted, her voice clear and alert despite the early hour. "We know all about that, and we're working on it. I'm so glad you're there. I thought you were going to Paris. But never mind. I need you to get over to city hall the minute it opens, to protest Metcom's application for demolition. Salvador will meet you there. Don't delay, dear. Metcom has a reputation for moving quickly once a deal is signed, and the word is that they have an appointment with the city engineers for this morning. Where have you been all weekend? I've tried and tried to reach you since I received my copy of *The Bugle* Saturday morning."

"*The Bugle*? Mother, what . . . ?"

"Your column's what alerted me. Thank God for that. It's a good thing you included that little bio of Matthew Fiedler at the end of your piece, darling, or his company might have gotten by with this. The minute I saw the name "Metcom," all sorts of alarm bells started ringing."

"But why?"

"Oh, Dee-Dee, if only you'd pay some attention to Embassy Holdings' activities. Metcom is a development company. If they're in town—any town—then trouble is sure to follow, so I began checking, which was not an easy matter over the weekend. I learned, though, that Chang International had been negotiating with Metcom to sell the Westmarch as part of a larger parcel of land. They signed the final papers late Friday afternoon.

"I feared, and rightly, it seems, for the Westmarch, because it's Metcom's policy to buy up crumbling neighborhoods, plow everything under, and start fresh."

Dee could hear Matt's voice. "Why can't we start

fresh, Dee?" Desperately, she clung to her mother's voice to block out the memory.

"That's not a bad thing, essentially," Helen continued, "but the problem is, they cut too wide a swath, and don't merely raze the crumbling areas. I'm sure that as they see it, if they leave the Westmarch standing, it will spoil the view for tenants of their new buildings." She gave a delicate, ladylike little snort. "People like that never understand that a building such as the Westmarch *is* a view. They've committed vandalism of that nature in other cities, and there's no reason to suspect they don't mean to do it here." She made a *tsk!* sound and went on.

"I told you they move quickly, and so must we. I'd be against their having the building even if you didn't live in it, darling. Maybe when Metcom learns that we intend to throw all kinds of obstacles in their path, they'll agree to selling us the place at a fair price. It's but a small portion of their overall purchase from Chang."

There was a smile in her voice. "That's why we called out the Action Committee. After all, what good will the building do them, if they're not permitted to carry out their intentions?"

She spoke at length, filling her daughter in.

After hanging up, Dee dialed again, and this time, instead of saying that there was no reply in Mr. Fiedler's room, the switchboard operator said brightly, "Mr. Fiedler has checked out."

Dee closed her eyes and lay back on her bed, feeling hot, slow tears trickle into her hair.

"Matt." Edwin's eyes glittered coldy in his heavy face. "Come in. Sit down." Edwin did not sit.

Matt shook his head, declining the seat. "Tell me what happened, Edwin. You said there was trouble. Big trouble. Shouldn't we have the rest of the team in on this?"

"No!" A silver coffeepot bounced as Edwin slammed his hand onto a rosewood table. "By God, I thought of it! I wanted each and every one of them to see what happens to a lily-livered sneak when he sells my company down the river! I—"

"What?" Matt could scarcely believe this. He'd seen Edwin angry before, but never like this. And never at him. "Suppose you tell me exactly what the hell is going on here, Edwin. I take it you're accusing me of something?"

"Accusing? You're bloody right, I'm accusing. I'm doing more than that! I'm—" He drew a deep breath and made a visible effort to control his temper. "Matt, I trusted you. It's only because I hold—held—you in the highest regard that I chose to keep this meeting private. But you betrayed that trust."

"I've never betr—"

"You have. You did. And before I bring the rest of the team in on this to plan damage control prior to going to city hall, I want to know for my own satisfaction exactly why you did it."

"Did what?" Matt all but shouted at his boss.

"Did what," Edwin snorted derisively. "Hell, I can understand a man getting hot for a woman, especially one who looks like this." He picked up a tabloid-sized newspaper that had been folded open, then folded in half again to display a column with a head-and-shoulders shot of Dee above it. "But to sell out your bread and butter for a piece of—"

"Watch it." Matt's tone was flat as he snatched the paper from Edwin's hand. "Hometown Tourist," he read. "By Dee Farris and . . . *Matthew Fiedler?*" He groaned, sat down hard on the chair, and covered his face with the palm of one hand. "Oh, Dee, you didn't!"

"Damn right she did!" Edwin grabbed the paper back and poked a blunt-tipped finger at the bottom of the column. 'Dee Farris,'" he read aloud, "'is a city business-woman whose column appears in every issue of *The Bugle*. Matthew Fiedler, an attorney with Metcom, Inc., a Toronto-based development group, collaborated with Ms. Farris on this piece during a recent business trip to the city.'"

"But . . ." Matt shook his head. He was stunned not only by Dee's having added his name to hers in the byline, but by Edwin's reaction to it. "Dammit," he said in confusion, "that column wasn't supposed to run until next week."

"Right!" Edwin slapped the paper on the back of a chair. "Exactly! It was supposed to run next week. Next week, when my plans had fallen through because of this protest. When I'd gone back to Toronto, beaten by some local chapter of the saviors of everything, never knowing of your complicity."

Matt focused on one word. "Protest?"

Edwin shot him a look of pure disgust. "Spare me the innocent act, Matt. We both know of your fondness for moldering edifices. That in itself is a conflict of interest that's long concerned me, but I always relied on your integrity. However, sleeping with that woman on the sly, discussing my business with her, was more than a minor conflict of interest. It was—"

"Dammit, Edwin!" Matt shot to his feet. "With all due respect, you have gone too far! Certainly, on the surface of things, my association with Dee might be seen as a conflict of interest, though a minor one. I didn't tell you that I was personally acquainted with one of the tenants in the Westmarch because I had no intention of telling *her* that the company I work for was negotiating to buy the place."

"Matt, I'm not stupid. I know about pillow talk. I know—"

"You know nothing! You're assuming. I did not tell Dee we had bought the property, not even that we were considering it!" Matt met Edwin's angry stare with one equally incensed. "My conscience is clear. My name appearing in that column in no way compromises me."

"Like hell it doesn't!" Edwin roared, slamming his hand onto the table again, setting dishes and silver to jangling. "Dammit! Even as we speak, there's a picket line in front of the Westmarch! It's been there, nonstop, since noon Saturday. They're the kind of picketers newspapers love, a bunch of righteously indignant blue-haired matrons, pipe-smoking old men, young women pushing baby carriages. They're out in force, demanding that the city 'save' the Westmarch from 'eastern rapists.' Us, Matt. Me. My company! How do you explain those pickets if they weren't hired by your girlfriend?"

Matt rammed a hand through his hair. "I can't explain it. All I can do is assure you I'm not responsible, and neither is Dee."

"Yes, you damned well are! You and your girlfriend. And don't try to tell me she doesn't have an ax to grind, because I know she does. Not only does she have a shop on the premises and occupy the penthouse suite, she—"

"I tell you, Edwin," Matt interrupted, driving one fist into the opposite palm, "Dee didn't even know the building was for sale. Dammit, she's been pouring money into it, making improvements to her boutique, enlarging. Would she be doing that if she knew the place was up for sale?"

"Damn right she would, because she believes she can stop me. She's going to block my every attempt to obtain a demolition permit. She knows that without it, the property's useless to me and—"

"A *what*?" Matt took a step toward Edwin. "A demolition permit?" The older man backed up a pace. "That building was merely to be renovated, not torn down! That was my recommendation. And the architect's. Even the Chang people were reluctant to include it, because of your reputation. Isn't that mainly why you agreed to save it, Edwin? You did agree!" Remnants of his nightmare flashed across his mind.

"Oh, hell! Why do you have advisers if you won't take our advice? If you've applied for a demolition permit, no wonder there are picketers at the building! Things like that can't be kept quiet! Nor should they be. That building is sound as well as old and beautiful. It's a city landmark. It should have been declared a heritage site years ago, but somehow it must have slipped through the cracks."

He leaned on the table with both hands as he begged. "It's not too late, Edwin. We can stop this, get rid of the picketers by canceling the application. We can make you look like a hero in this city. There's no need to destroy the Westmarch. Incorporate it into the new development the way Karl and I suggested from the beginning. Dammit, what the hell changed your mind? Or were you lying to me all along simply to shut me up?"

Edwin's jowls jiggled. "It's in my way. And it's just a

building, Matt. A pile of stones. In the whole scheme of things what can it matter? For one thing it doesn't meet earthquake standards. It—" He broke off and waved his hand dismissively.

"This is all beside the point, and I have no intention of debating it with you. It's not your concern. The building belongs to me. I will do whatever I think is right. And you will get—"

Edwin's teeth clacked shut as a knock sounded at the door. Striding across the room, he yanked it open. The bell captain stood there, and the day manager. The latter spoke. "Mr. Fiedler's bags have been packed as requested, Mr. James. Shall I hold them downstairs for you?"

Edwin's head bobbed once. "Very good. Mr. Fiedler will be down presently. Have his ticket waiting, and a taxi at the door. That will be all." He shut the door with a decisive thud.

"I've seen to your checkout, Matt. By the time you arrive in Toronto, your personal effects will have been removed from your office, and the condo will be closed. The receptionist will be able to tell you where your belongings from both have been stored."

He paused. "There will be no letter of recommendation."

He swung the door open, stood staring at Matt coldly. "That will be all," he said, dismissing Matt, an employee of nearly ten years, as easily as he'd dismissed the hotel personnel.

Matt reeled. "Edwin. Are you saying I'm fired? Without cause? Without proof of complicity? That column of Dee's is nothing more than circumstantial evidence and has nothing to do with the pickets. It's your damned demolition application that brought them out."

"I haven't made it yet. We have an appointment at city hall for later this morning."

Matt shook his head. "Haven't made it yet? But . . . Dammit, I don't understand. I—"

"Understand this." Edwin's voice was as steely as his glare. "I do not keep in my employ a man I cannot trust. I give every man one chance. But I never give him two. Get out; and be damned grateful I'm not having you disbarred for this."

Matt stepped out into the corridor, then turned and placed his palm against the door, preventing Edwin's closing it. "You're wrong about this," he said. "I don't know how to prove it to you, but you are. I'll go, because you leave me no choice, but there is another explanation. I hope someday you find it."

For a moment Edwin appeared to falter, but then he lifted his head another half-inch and said, "If I'm wrong about all this, son, then I'm wrong about something else as well. I never pegged you as being any woman's dupe, but I suppose that's a possibility. Behind those picketers is a company with a number of divisions. One of those divisions buys up old buildings in cities around the world, renovates them, and donates them to heritage societies, or city or state governments. It's a tax dodge. That company, Matt, is Embassy Holdings. Owned by two women. Lady Helen Farris, and her daughter, Dee."

As Matt's hand fell from the door, Edwin closed it in his face. Matt didn't notice. He was hearing an echo of the words "woman's dupe."

"No," he said aloud. Dammit, no. If he'd been duped, it was by Edwin James.

It was easier now to understand Edwin's suggestion that Matt miss the final meeting with Chang International. Easier to make sense of Edwin's recommendation that Matt return to Toronto for a weekend of R & R. Undoubtedly, if he'd gone, Edwin would have found something to keep him occupied there. He'd wanted to escape a battle with Matt over destroying the Westmarch. He wondered what Edwin had thought, learning that Matt preferred to stay, that he had a date for Friday evening? He hadn't mentioned his hopes for Saturday and Sunday, hopes that had been more than fulfilled. Maybe Edwin's hopes, too, had been fulfilled by Matt's disappearance over the weekend. He wondered what those telephone messages would have said had he taken the time to listen. *Matt, go home? Matt, you're off the job?*

And what the hell did it matter now? He was off the job all right. Permanently.

Shouldering himself away from the wall, Matt went down to the lobby to collect his bags.

Dee fought her way through the crowd of protesting citizens and was forced to employ her best duchess manner to get past the city-hall receptionist and into council chambers. As a tenant in the Westmarch, she had a right to be heard, and she intended to exercise it.

As she entered, she was surprised—and relieved—to discover Matt was not there.

A large, florid man had the floor as he stood and addressed the mayor, who leaned forward, listening attentively. ". . . and I resent being forced into this time-wasting session, Mayor," he was saying as Dee slipped into a chair. "I came this morning to meet, not with you and your council, as honored as I am by your august presence, but with the city engineers and building inspectors, to discuss the advisability of attempting to renovate the Westmarch Apartment Hotel, which I had recently bought."

The mayor raised her eyebrows. "Forgive me for disagreeing, Mr. James, but my information is that your meeting with the city engineering department this morning was to make application for a demolition permit applicable to the Westmarch Apartment Hotel."

Well! Maybe this wasn't going to be the cakewalk Metcom—and Matt—had thought it would be. Was that why Matt wasn't there? Because he'd not thought he needed to bother? Dee let out a long breath she hadn't been aware of holding. Before she could draw it back in, the door opened, Matt came into the room, and she forget about such functions as breathing.

His eyes seemed to find her as if by some kind of magnetism. Shock, disbelief, flooded his face. Of course. He thought she was safely out of the way for a week. Seeing her there must be a mighty jolt for him. For a long moment they stared at each other. Then, as Metcom's CEO began speaking again, Matt sank onto a chair across the aisle from Dee.

Dee remembered to breathe. The pain of it made her sway and grip the back of the chair in front of her.

Matt saw Dee's face pale as he walked in. He saw her knuckles turn white. He saw her swallow. Saw the rage, the hatred, in her eyes. Why was she there? Why hadn't she gotten on that plane? Oh, Lord, she thought he was part of this! What else could she think? He wanted to go to her, tell her he'd known nothing of the planned demolition but . . . how could he?

Hell, he knew how Metcom worked. He'd known all along how unlikely it was that Edwin would listen to him and Karl this time, when five times out of eight, he'd failed to before. He'd blinded himself to the truth because he'd hated to think of the outcome if Edwin was simply "going along" until he had everything signed and sealed.

He closed his eyes and listened to Edwin drone on

about how they had sought the permit only as a precautionary measure, so that he—and city hall—would not be inconvenienced by the very kind of vociferous and self-seeking protests they were being subjected to now. Of course Metcom wouldn't use the permit unless the final survey of the building proved it basically unsafe, Edwin claimed.

And without Matt there to make sure that everything was straight and aboveboard, what guarantee was there that Edwin wouldn't find someone to declare the building unsafe?

It was ironic, wasn't it? He'd lost Dee because of his job; he'd lost his job because of Dee. And without that job, he could do nothing to win back Dee's trust.

"Metcom, Inc., has done many fine things for many cities in this country and abroad," Edwin was saying when Matt listened again. He opened his eyes and fixed his gaze on Dee's profile, willing her to look at him.

She did not.

"We have every hope of doing the same for this one," Edwin said, all eager sincerity. "Your city's unemployment rate is higher than the national average. The four stages of our proposed development will help alleviate that problem by providing three hundred man-years of work prior to its completion. Those are direct job benefits, Mayor. Then there are the spin-offs, as I'm sure you must be aware, in the service industries."

Dee saw the mayor exchange glances with several

members of council. Her heart sank. In times of unemployment job creation bought votes. She bit her lower lip so hard, she tasted blood. She felt Matt's eyes on her, closed hers, and knew she was going to cry.

She would not, could not, do it here. She stood, ignoring the startled glance Salvador, the Embassy Holdings lawyer, gave her. As Edwin James began exhorting the mayor not to let "unwashed malcontents" stop "progress," she stumbled past the aisle where Matt was sitting, and toward the door, which seemed a mile away.

The mayor's voice, sounding irritated, followed Dee out the door, stating unequivocally that she was swayed neither by protests nor by entrepreneurial eloquence. Her decisions were based on facts. . . .

Unsure if the mayor's words meant good news or bad, Dee followed a corridor blindly until it came to an end, thrust her head against a fire door, and found herself outside in the rain. It didn't matter. Rain couldn't hurt her. Head down, arms wrapped around herself, she paced along a leaf-littered walkway.

She bumped into a stone bench, noticed that it was dry, stared at it for a minute, then sat on its cold surface, leaning on the wall behind her. Now that she was alone, where she might be able to find the release of tears, they refused to come. Her eyes, dry, burning, gazed straight ahead, staring at Captain George Vancouver's bronze, guano-dribbled shoulders.

Into her field of view came a large, tanned hand.

Dangling from it was a set of keys. Hers. She snatched them, stood, and strode away without once looking at Matt. She had no idea where her car was. It didn't matter. What mattered was getting away from him. Escaping the pain.

Surprisingly, she found her car without a search, across the street from city hall. She drove straight home, wondering for how much longer she would have a home. That, she realized, didn't matter a whole lot either.

She got through that first night. She got through the next five nights. And the intervening days. It amazed her to hear herself talking intelligently to the staff in her boutiques, answering queries from customers, apologizing to the designers she had intended to meet with in France. She spoke to her mother, chattering about inconsequential topics. She never asked about the status of the battle. Her mother never volunteered.

Once or twice Dee even laughed, and that, too, sounded quite normal while feeling alien.

She waited, daily, for the eviction notice. Discussed the situation with Jenkins, with the day doorman, commiserated with both on the upcoming loss of their jobs.

Saturday she picked vegetables in the hydroponic gardens for Jenkins, sent them down in the elevator, and then stood still for a long time, smelling the warm, sweet earth in which her jungle plants grew. She forced herself to move and put up new cuttlebones for the birds. She tossed beads of food to the koi in the pond and listened to the splashing of the little waterfall, then went back inside.

In the kitchen she found herself standing very still again, as if she were waiting for something. She glanced at the microwave. Had she put a frozen dinner in it? It was empty. Had she eaten? She stood very still while she wondered about that.

She heard Jenkins send the elevator back up. She heard the macaw scream, and frowned, looking toward the door. The bead curtain, visible through the archway, parted, and suddenly Dee's knees gave way. She sat down abruptly on a stool and stared at Matt as he walked toward her.

His hair was beaded with moisture. His face was thin, drawn, taut. He looked pale, but his hands were as large as ever. He carried two white boxes stacked one on top of the other. From them emanated the pungent, unmistakable odor of Montreal smoked meat.

Dee's mouth watered. So did her eyes. She swallowed and blinked.

"Hi," he said.

"Hi." It was a thin, scratchy thread of sound. She swallowed and said, "Welcome home."

As if he hadn't heard her, Matt said, "I bribed Jenkins." He set the boxes on the counter. "With one of these." He folded back the lid of one, lifted out a sandwich wrapped in a plain white bag, and offered it to her. She bit into it. She closed her eyes again.

Matt leaned on the other side of the counter and flipped up the lid on the other box. Silently, not looking at each other, they ate their sandwiches, their pickles. Dee licked mustard off one finger. She rose and went to the fridge. His beer was still there.

She poured two and slid one along the counter to him. He drank deeply, set the glass down, and looked at her. Waiting.

She picked up the boxes to put into the garbage and saw the writing on the lids. The restaurant's name. Its address. Its phone number. They even did takeout.

She drew a deep breath. "Why . . . ?" Her voice cracked, but before she could regroup and finish her sentence, he spoke.

Shoving his hands into his raincoat pockets, he shrugged, his eyes narrowed as if he were in pain. "How could I have done anything else? I had to ask myself where my loyalty lay. With the woman I love, or with the man who paid my salary? It wasn't an easy decision. The best I could do was try to ensure that this place would survive. I did try to do that. If I'd quit my job at Metcom, as I considered doing, as I would have had to if I wanted to warn you, then you . . . the Westmarch would have had no protection."

His hard mouth quirked in a half-smile. "Or so I

thought. I wasn't aware of Embassy Holdings' Heritage Division, or the power it wields."

His smile widened a fraction, and for a moment his flinty eyes softened. "She's some woman, your mother. I begin to see what you might be like thirty years from now. She offered me a job. I was tempted to take it. But . . ." He shrugged as if to say he was content with the job he had.

He shook one of his hands free and unbuttoned his coat to get at his suit jacket. From an inner pocket he withdrew a legal-size envelope and slid it toward her.

Dee took it warily, her eyes on his face, then reluctantly looked down so she could open it. Unfolding its contents, she squinted at the ornate calligraphy that proclaimed it to be a deed. The plain type, though, listed the Westmarch Apartment Hotel as the property of Embassy Holdings, Heritage Division. It was signed by Edwin James, and by her mother, in the city of Victoria, as of today's date.

Dee closed her eyes. "How . . . ?" She opened them again and saw Matt disappearing through the bead curtain. "No!" she cried. "Matt! Wait."

He turned, looked at her, and waited. She drew in a deep breath and let it out slowly. "Matt, when I asked you why, I wasn't asking why you didn't tell me what Metcom planned. I know why. I figured it out quite soon. You're underestimating me again. This time my capacity to understand business ethics, your personal integrity. Did you think I'd be unable to see that if you'd broken your employer's trust, you'd have been unable to respect yourself? That even if you'd quit your job with him, and then told me his plans, you'd have been morally in the wrong? I knew that, too, I know it . . . here." She touched her heart. "As well as you do."

He frowned, rubbing a finger along the groove between his brows. "Then what . . . ?"

"What was I asking 'why' for? Because you'd left the sandwiches in their boxes. Because you were giving me the address."

He lifted a hand and touched her face. "You know the answer to that too. It's time for me to go, Dee. I come to say good-bye, kid."

Dee stared at him, fighting against the ache in her throat. "You left me once before and lied, saying you'd be back. No lies this time, Matt?"

He shook his head again. "No lies this time, Dee."

"But you're still walking."

He nodded.

"This is one answer I don't know. Why, Matt?"

"Because I have no job. Hell, I don't even have a home. I'm in the same boat as my father when he lost his job. My home was a company house, too, and that's gone. My most priceless assets are a couple of oil paintings. It's not enough, Dee. Not enough for me. To want to give you."

She held his gaze. "You do have one thing, though, don't you, Matt?"

"What's that?"

"Pride," she said with a shrug as she turned away. "Enjoy it."

This time it was he who reached out. He took her arm and spun her around. There was anger in his eyes. And pain. And . . . hope? "You walked away too, Dee. You gave me no chance to explain. No chance to tell you . . . anything."

"I know. And I'm sorry." She would never forget the confusion of that day she hadn't gone to Paris. She didn't think she could explain it. Nor did she think she really had to. That was one of the good things about love. "If I'd given you a chance to talk, what would you have told me, Matt?"

His misery was almost tangible to her. She couldn't relieve it. He had to do that himself. "I don't know," he said. "Maybe that I was sorry too. Maybe that I love you. Maybe that . . . someday . . ."

She shook her head. "No, Matt. Not someday."

"Okay." He shrugged. He was going to leave.

"Matt. I have another question. Why didn't you take off your coat?"

"What?"

"When you came in. You stood there. You brought me dinner. You didn't sit down. And you didn't take off your coat."

"I wasn't invited to."

"Do you require that kind of invitation in your own home?"

He stared at her. "It isn't my home."

"It's mine, Matt. If you had one and I didn't, would you expect me to wait for an invitation? I said, 'Welcome home.' I meant it. What do you think love is all about, Matt? Will you spend the rest of your life running from me because I'm rich, or trying to play catch-up so you'll feel you qualify?"

His mouth compressed. A white line appeared around his nose. "Dammit, Dee. What do you want from me?"

Dee sighed. "Everything, Matt. Your life. Your love. Your future." She hesitated, lifted her chin, and added softly, "Your children. Even your name, if you're willing to share it."

He drew her to within inches of his body. She felt his heat, smelled his scent. Sensed his need. "I won't live on your money."

She shrugged, and his hands were so heavy on her shoulders, she lifted them only an inch. "So earn your own."

"I won't always be polite in polite society. If I have to meet your titled relatives, I might blow it entirely."

"That's okay. Polite society isn't always. As for titled relatives, they can fend for themselves."

"I won't let you retreat to your own side of the bed."

"I've grown up enough not to want to, Matt."

"I won't ever stop being jealous of that son of a bitch, Dee. If I ever meet him, I'm going to break his jaw."

Dee smiled. "With a baseball bat?"

He pulled her tightly against him. Held her. They both trembled and clung to each other as if they'd been hanging from the side of a cliff and had now found safety.

Dee tilted a radiant face to him. "What else won't you do?" she asked.

"I won't let you go," he said roughly. "Not ever."

EPILOGUE

Matt paused on his way up the marble stairs under the green-and-white canopy. Jenkins saw him approach and strode stiffly across the lobby. Matt didn't wait, using his key and thrusting open the door before the old man arrived.

His smile was softly proud as he brushed his sleeve over the gilt lettering on the heavy beveled glass. THE WESTMARCH HOUSE, it read on one line, followed by EMBASSY HOLDINGS: HERITAGE DIVISION HEADQUARTERS. MATTHEW J. FIEDLER, DIRECTOR.

Dee arrived then, slipping through the door that separated the retail lobby from the residential. Sliding her arm around his waist, she lifted her face for his kiss.

"Where are the kids?" he asked.

"Mom's taken them shopping. Cynthia's determined

to have something strapless for the reception tonight. Mark's almost as determined to wear jeans."

"Hmm. Before Cynthia goes strapless, she's going to have to produce something to hold a dress up."

Dee nodded as Jenkins keyed the elevator for them. "She will, darling. Sooner than you will like, I expect."

"Do you expect your mother will have the kids back here sooner than I'll like?" he asked as they entered the solarium, smelling the sweet earth, exotic flowers, and tomato plants. Overhead, a red macaw swooped and shrieked.

Dee smiled at Matt. "That depends on what you have in mind."

He thrust aside the bamboo curtain, slid open the glass door, and rushed her inside. Picking her up in his arms, he said, "For what I have in mind, it would be much better if your mother kept the kids with her in her suite downstairs tonight."

Dee tilted her head consideringly. "Well, I suppose that could be arranged. After all, how often do you and I get to spend a night in town all alone? Since Mom did say something about leaving the reception early, and since the children are only eight and nine years of age, it would only be appropriate if she takes them with her when she makes her excuses. And it is your night, so, yes, I think we can manage to give you anything you want."

"Right," Matt said. "My tenth anniversary as director of the division. And I can have anything I want?"

And don't miss these heart-stopping
romances from Bantam Books,
on sale in October:

OUTLAW by Susan Johnson

MOONLIGHT, MADNESS,
AND MAGIC
by Suzanne Forster,
Charlotte Hughes,
and Olivia Rupprecht

SATIN AND STEELE
by Fayrene Preston

And in hardcover from Doubleday:

SOMETHING BORROWED,
SOMETHING BLUE
by Gillian Karr

ILLEGAL MOTION, LOVESWEPT #651, is as good as they come. Football star Nick Logan was desperate enough to try anything to clear his name, and he figured he could intimidate or charm the truth out of Willa Trask—until he was burned by the sparks that flared between him and the beautiful redhead! He'd hired her to rehabilitate his injured knee, vowing to discover if she'd helped frame him—but instead of an ice princess, he found in her a wanton witch who touched his soul. When you've read this winning story, I'm sure you'll become big fans of Donna Kauffman!

We turn from a rookie to an all-star pro for our next Dangerous Man. Let the heartbreaking emotion of Laura Taylor sweep you away with **WILDER'S WOMAN**, LOVESWEPT #652. Craig Wilder—uncivilized, untamed, he'd paid a high price for survival. He'd meant to teach Chelsea Lockridge a lesson, to punish his ex-wife for her betrayal, but he hadn't anticipated the erotic torment of molding his body to hers—nor imagined the tenderness still buried deep inside his battered heart! She'd braved the wilderness and a storm with evidence that could deliver the justice Craig had been denied, but Chelsea wanted to prove she'd never lost faith in him . . . or her reckless passion for the man who could make her purr with pleasure. Branded for all eternity by a lover whose scars ran deep, she vowed she could help Craig mourn the past and trust her again by fighting his demons with the sweet fury of her love. Laura's deeply moving tale will capture you, heart and soul.

If you like your men *truly* dangerous, Glenna McReynolds has the mystery man for you in **AVENG-ING ANGEL**, LOVESWEPT #653. Bruised and bloody, Dylan Jones has driven a thousand miles with her name on his lips, desperate to save Johanna Lane from being murdered! The secrets she knew made her a target, and he was her best chance of getting out alive—even if it meant abducting the lady and keeping her with him against her will. Frightened and furious, Johanna was stunned to realize she knew her captor . . . and once had even desired him! Dylan gambled his life to feel her heat and taste the forbidden fruit of her lips and Johanna longed to repay the debt. I can't think of a better way to end your month of **DANGEROUS MEN** than with Glenna's **AVENGING ANGEL**!

So hang on to your hearts—next month six **DANGEROUS MEN** are coming to steal them away!

Happy reading,

Nita Taublib

Nita Taublib

Associate Publisher

P.S. Don't miss the exciting women's fiction Bantam has coming in November—sensual seduction in Susan Johnson's **OUTLAW**; love and black magic over the centuries in **MOONLIGHT, MADNESS, AND MAGIC** by LOVESWEPT authors Suzanne Forster, Charlotte Hughes, and Olivia Rupprecht; and a classic Fayrene Preston romance, **SATIN AND STEELE**. We'll be giving you a sneak peek at these terrific books in next month's LOVESWEPTs. And immediately following this page, look for a preview of the spectacular women's fiction books from Bantam *available now!*

Don't miss these exciting books by your
favorite Bantam authors

On sale in September:
A WHISPER OF ROSES
by *Teresa Medeiros*

TENDER BETRAYAL
by *Rosanne Bittner*

THE PAINTED LADY
by *Lucia Grahame*

OREGON BROWN
by *Sara Orwig*

And in hardcover from Doubleday
SEIZED BY LOVE
by *Susan Johnson*

Teresa Medeiros

nationally bestselling author of
ONCE AN ANGEL
and HEATHER AND VELVET

presents

A WHISPER OF ROSES

"From humor to adventure, poignancy to passion,
tenderness to sensuality, Teresa Medeiros writes rare
love stories to cherish."—*Romantic Times*

*Set in the wild Highlands of Scotland, this captivating
historical romance is bursting with the breathtaking passion,
sparkling humor, and enchanting atmosphere that have
made Teresa Medeiros a bestselling author. It tells the
heartbreaking tale of two lovers torn between their passion
and the clan rivalry that divides their families.*

The door behind him crashed open into the opposite wall,
and Morgan swung around to find himself facing yet
another exotic creature of myth.

A princess, her cloud of dark hair tumbled loose around
her shoulders, the light behind her throwing every curve
beneath her ivory nightdress into magnificent relief. Her
delicate fingers were curled not around a scepter, but
around the engraved hilt of a ceremonial claymore.

Silvery fingers of moonlight caressed the five feet of
steel that lay between her hands and his heart.

"Hold your ground, rogue MacDonnell," she sweetly
snarled. "One careless step and I'll be forced to take your
head downstairs without the rest of you."

Morgan didn't even feel the pain as the crystal rose

snapped in his clumsy hands, embedding its stem deep in his palm.

"Why, you clumsy oaf! Look what you've gone and done now!"

Morgan's gaze automatically dropped to his hands. A jagged shard of glass protruded from his palm. Warm blood trickled down his wrist and forearm to puddle on one of Elizabeth Cameron's precious rugs. Before he could quench it, the old shame flared. Shame for being a MacDonnell. Shame for being such a crude ox. Just as quickly on its heels followed rage—the crushing rage that shielded his tattered pride from every blow. But before he could unleash it on the hapless girl, she dropped the sword and rushed over to him.

Tossing the splintered remains of the rose aside without a second glance, she cradled his hand in hers and dabbed at the wound with a wad of her nightdress. Her little hand was warm and soft and silky smooth beneath his own. "You really should take more care," she chided. "If you'd have struck your wrist, you might have bled to death."

Morgan was too dumbfounded by her concern to point out her illogic. If she'd have cut off his head, he might have bled to death even quicker. Still scowling over his hand, she dragged him toward the pale circle of light at the window.

"Be very still," she commanded. "I'm going to try to fish out this piece of glass. It's bound to be painful. You may scream if you like. I shan't think any less of you."

Since she'd never thought much of him to begin with, Morgan wasn't concerned. He didn't even flinch when she pressed his palm with her thumb and snagged the sliver of glass between the polished crescents of her fingernails.

Thoroughly bemused, Morgan studied her in the moonlight. The top of her head barely came to his chest. The spiral curls he used to yank with such relish tumbled down her back in inky waves. Her skin was fair except for the faintest hint of color, as if God had brushed rose petals across her cheeks and lips. A fringe of ebony silk shuttered her eyes. Her scent filled his nostrils, and he was shocked to feel his throat tighten with a primal hunger. She smelled like her mother, but fresher, sweeter. Some primitive male instinct warned him this was a bloom still on the vine, fragrant and tender and ripe. He frowned. She might be nectar to another man, but to him, Dougal Cameron's daughter would be as deadly as nightshade.

Her teeth cut into her lower lip as if to bite back a cry of her own as she drew forth the shard of glass and stanched the bleeding with yet another wad of her nightdress. Morgan feared he might soon have more of it twined around his arm than she had around her body. But an intriguing glimpse of a slender calf silenced his protest.

Grimacing, she lay the bloody splinter on the window-sill before glancing up at him.

At that moment, he cocked his head to the side, giving her an unobstructed view of his face. Moonlight melted over its harsh planes and angles, etching its alien virility in ruthless lines. He was a stranger, yet so hauntingly familiar she couldn't stop her hand from lifting, her fingertips from brushing the stubborn jut of his jaw. His eyes were guarded, like the forest at dusk.

"Hello, brat," he said.

Then she felt that old, familiar kick in the stomach and knew she was standing face to face in the moonlit tower with Morgan MacDonnell, his boyish promise of masculine beauty come to devastating fruition.

Mortified by her own boldness, she snatched her hand back, remembering another time she had touched him in tenderness and he had rubuked her in anger.

A wry grin touched his lips. "I suppose if you'd have known it was me, you'd have let me bleed to death."

Terrified she was going to revert to a stammering six-year-old, she snapped, "Of course not. You were dripping all over Mama's Flemish rug."

To hide her consternation, she lowered her gaze back to his hand. That was a mistake for she could not help staring, fascinated by the blunt size of his fingers, the warmth of his work-roughened skin, the rhythmic throb of his pulse beneath her thumb. She had the absurd thought that it must take a mighty heart indeed to fuel such a man.

"You've grown," she blurted out accusingly.

"So have you."

His low, amused tone warned her. She looked up to find his gaze taking a leisurely jaunt up her body, finally coming to rest with bold regard on her face. A splinter of anger twisted in her heart. For so long she had yearned for him to look at her with affection. But why now, when she sensed his admiration might be even more lethal to her than enmity?

Hardly aware of her actions, she tore a strip of priceless Chinese silk from her mother's drapes and wrapped it around his palm. "So what were you doing up here? Plotting a massacre? Trying to find a way to lower the harpsichord out the window? Searching for a mouse to put in my bed?"

Lucky mouse, Morgan thought, but he wisely refrained from saying so. "If you must know, lass, I was searchin' for a moment's peace."

"Ha!" She knotted the bandage with a crisp jerk that finally drew a flinch from him. "Peace and the MacDonnells hardly go hand in hand."

"Fine talk from a lass who just burst in here threatenin' to cut off my head."

Sabrina could hardly argue with the truth of that.

He jerked his head toward the door. "Why aren't you down there with the rest of your family, lordin' your noble gestures over the poor peasants?"

Morgan's size might have changed, but not the rest of him. Resenting his uncanny knack of making her feel ashamed of who she was, she gave a dainty snort. "Peasants, indeed. Barefoot savages, the lot of them. Mama would have been better off serving them at a trough instead of a table."

His voice was quiet, its very lack of emotion a rebuke of its own. "If their table manners aren't to your likin', it might be because most of them won't see that much food again in their lifetimes. And their feet are bare because they're savin' the rotted soles of their boots for the cold winter months. They don't lose as many toes that way."

Shame buffeted her. Sabrina dropped her gaze, then wished she hadn't as it fell on the stark lines of Morgan's bare legs and feet. Golden hair dusted his muscular calves. His soles must be as tough as leather to bear the stony soil of the mountainside without protection. Her own toes curled sheepishly into the plush cashmere of her stockings.

"I begged Mama to let me join the festivities," she confessed.

"Why didn't you appeal to your dotin' papa? As I recall,

he never could resist a flutter of those pretty little lashes of yours."

Sabrina's gaze shot to his face. Morgan had never given her any indication that he'd noticed her lashes before. "Even Papa was adamant this time." A soft chuckle escaped her. "It seems your reputations preceded you. He was terrified one of you might hit me over the head and drag me off by my hair."

Morgan was silent for so long that she feared she'd offended him again. Then he reached down and lifted a skein of her hair in his uninjured hand, rubbing it between thumb and forefinger. A dreamy languor stole across her features. The cadence of Sabrina's heartbeat shifted in warning.

He let the stolen tendril ripple through his fingers in a cascade of midnight silk before turning the dusky heat of his gaze on her. "I can't say I blame him, lass. If you were mine, I'd probably lock you away, too."

If you were mine . . .

The words hung suspended between them, far more awkward than their silence. In a breath of utter lunacy, Sabrina wondered how it would feel to belong to a man like him, dared to ponder what came after being dragged off by her hair.

Caught in the same spell of moonlight and solitude, Morgan's gaze dropped to her parted lips. His starving senses reeled, intoxicated by the scent of roses that flared his nostrils, the cling of her hair against his callused knuckles. He'd long ago resigned himself to the harsh life of a Highland warrior. But this girl's softness awakened old hungers and weakened his resolve. He hadn't touched a drop of wine, yet he felt drunk, reckless. What harm could one kiss to? Resisting the temptation to plunge his tongue between her unwitting lips, he leaned down and touched his mouth to hers.

At the press of Morgan's lips against her own, Sabrina's eyes fluttered shut. His kiss was brief, dry, almost tentative, yet a melting sweetness unfolded within her. She felt the leashed power in his touch. Such gentleness in a man his size wove a spell all its own. Only in the last brief second of contact did he allow himself the wicked luxury of dragging his lips across hers, molding her beneath him in perfect harmony.

TENDER BETRAYAL
by
ROSANNE BITTNER

Bestselling author of OUTLAW HEARTS
and THUNDER ON THE PLAINS

"Bittner's characters are so finely drawn, their lives so
richly detailed, one cannot help but to care deeply for
each of them." —*Affaire de Coeur*

*When Audra Brennan savored her first, forbidden taste of
desire in the arms of handsome lawyer Lee Jeffreys, his
caresses sparked a flame within that burned away the differences between rebel and Yankee.*

The shelling from the bigger guns seemed to have
stopped. She decided that at least until daylight she had no
choice but to stay here as Lee had directed. She went back
to the cot and lay down, breathing his scent on his pillow
and sheets. How odd that she felt so safe in this bed where
a Yankee soldier slept. She was in the center of the enemy
camp, yet she was not afraid.

She drifted off to sleep, losing all track of time. Finally
someone knocked gently on the rear door. "Audra? It's
me."

Audra rubbed at her eyes, holding the shirt around
herself as she found her way to the door. It was still dark.
"Lee?"

"Let me in. The worst is over."

Audra obeyed, and Lee turned and latched the door
again. Audra looked up at him, seeing blood on his right
arm. "You're hurt!"

"Nothing drastic. I told my commander I'd tend to it

myself. He doesn't know you're in here, and I don't want him to know just yet." He threw a bundle of clothes on the small table on which the lamp was sitting. "I looted those out of a clothing store like a common thief. I don't know your size. I just took a guess. You've got to have something to wear when you leave here."

Lee removed his jacket and boots, then began unbuttoning his shirt. "It's a madhouse out there. Most of the men have chased the rebels back into the countryside, and they're looting through town like crazy men. It's practically impossible to keep any of these men in line. They aren't regular army, just civilian volunteers, for the most part, come here to teach the rebels a lesson. They don't know a damn thing about real military conduct or how to obey orders." He glanced at her. "I still intend to have the bastards who attacked you whipped. How do you feel?"

She sat down on the cot, suddenly self-conscious now that she was more rested. She had removed her shoes and stockings and wore only her shirt and her bloomers. "Just terribly tired and . . . I don't know . . . numb, I guess. It's all so ugly and unreal."

"That's war, Audra, ugly and unreal. You asked me once what it's like. Now you know." He peeled off his bloodstained shirt, and Audra found herself studying his muscular arms and the familiar broad chest, the dark hair that lightly dusted that chest and led downward in a V shape past the belt of his pants. He walked to the stand that still held a bowl of water and he poured some fresh water into it, then wet a rag and held it to the cut on his arm, which was already scabbing over. "Some rebel tried to stab me with his bayonet. Missed what he was aiming for by a long shot, but he didn't miss me all together, obviously."

"Let me help you."

"Don't worry about it. It isn't bleeding anymore." He washed his face and neck, then dried off and picked up a flask of whiskey. He opened it and poured some over the cut, grimacing at the sting of it. Then he swallowed some of the whiskey straight from the flask. "They say whiskey is supposed to help ease pain," he said then. "It does, but only physical pain. It doesn't do a thing for the pain in a man's heart."

She looked away. "Lee, don't—"

"Why not? In a couple of days you'll go back to Brennan Manor, and I'll go on with what I have to do, because I'm bound to do it and it isn't in me to be a deserter, no matter the reason. You have to stay near home because it's the only way you're going to know what happened to Joey, and you'll want to be there when he comes home, God willing. Who knows what will happen when all this is over? In the meantime I've found you again, and I need to tell you I love you, Audra. I never stopped loving you and I probably never will."

Audra held back tears. Why was he saying this now, when it was impossible for them to be together? Everything had changed. They were not the same people as they'd been that summer at Maple Shadows, and besides that, it was wrong to be sitting here half-undressed in front of the man she'd slept with while married to someone else, wasn't it? It was wrong to care this much about a Yankee. *All* of this was wrong, but then, what was right anymore?

He set the flask down on the table. "This might really be it, Audra; the end for you and me. But we have tonight."

"Why is it always that way for us? It was like that at Maple Shadows, and that one night you came to visit. All we ever have is one night, Lee, never knowing what will come tomorrow. I can't do that again. It hurts too much, and it's wrong."

Audra looked away as Lee began to undress. "Please take me somewhere, Lee, anywhere away from here."

He came over to kneel in front of her, grasping her wrists. "There *is* no place to take you, not tonight. And it's *not* wrong, Audra. It was *never* wrong, and you know it. And this time it isn't just tonight. When this is over, I'm coming back, and we're going to be together, do you hear me? I'm not going to live like this the rest of my life. I want you, Audra, and dammit, you want *me*! We've both known it since that first day you came here to see me, widow or not! Maybe this *is* the last chance we'll have to be together, but as God is my witness, if I don't get killed or so badly wounded that I can't come to you, I'll be back to find you, and we're going to put this war behind us!"

She looked at him pleadingly. "That's impossible now," she said in a near whisper.

"That isn't true. You just don't want to *believe* that it's possible, because it makes you feel like a traitor." He leaned closer. "Well, then, *I'm* a traitor, too! Because while my men are out there chasing and killing rebels, I'll be in here making *love* to one!"

Why couldn't she object, argue, remember why she should say no? Why was she never able to resist this man she should have hated?

"I never said anything about making love," she whispered.

He searched her green eyes, eyes that had told him all along how much she wanted him again. "You didn't have to," he answered.

THE PAINTED LADY
by
LUCIA GRAHAME

This is a stunningly sensual first novel about sexual awakening set in nineteenth-century France and England. Romantic Times *called it "a unique and rare reading experience."*

This wonderfully entertaining novel showcases the superb writing talents of Lucia Grahame. With lyric simplicity and beauty THE PAINTED LADY will entrance you from first page to last. Read on to discover an exquisite story about a proud, dark-haired woman and her hidden desire that is finally freed.

"If I stay longer with you tonight," Anthony said, his words seeming to reach me through a thick mist, "it will be on one condition. You will not balk at *anything* I ask of you. I leave it to you. I will go now and count tonight to your account, since, although you were occasionally dilatory, you acquitted yourself well enough, for the most part. Or I will stay, on *my* conditions—but at *your* wish. It rests with you. Do I stay or go?"

"Stay," I whispered.

I swayed and jingled as he led me back to the hearthside and laid me down upon the pillows.

"Undress me," he commanded when we were stretched out before the fire. "Slowly. As slowly as you can."

I moved closer to him and began to unfasten the buttons of his waistcoat.

He sighed.

"Don't rush," he whispered. "I can feel how eager you are, but try to control yourself. Take your time."

It was maddening to force myself to that unhurried

pace, but in the end it only sharpened my hunger. As I contemplated the climactic pleasures in store—who could have said how long it would take to achieve them?—I could not help savoring the small but no less sweet ones immediately at hand. The slight drag against my skin of the fine wool that clothed him, more teasing even than I had imagined it; the almost imperceptible fragrance of lavender that wafted from his shirt, the hands which lay so lightly upon my waist as I absorbed the knowledge that the task he had set for me was not an obstacle to fulfillment but a means of enhancing it.

Yet I had unbuttoned only his waistcoat and his shirt when he told me to stop. He drew back from me a little. The very aura of controlled desire he radiated made me long to submerge myself in the impersonal heat and forgetfulness that his still presence next to me both promised and withheld.

I moved perhaps a centimeter closer to him.

"No," he said.

He began, in his calm, unhasty way, to remove his remaining clothing himself. I steadied my breath a little and watched the firelight move like a sculptor's fingers over his cool, hard body.

At last he leaned over me, but without touching me.

"You're so compliant tonight," he said almost tenderly. "You must be very hungry for your freedom, *mon fleur du miel*."

I felt a twist of sadness. For an instant, I thought he had used Frederick's nickname for me. But he had called me something quite different—a flower, not of evil, but of sweetness . . . honey.

He brought his hand to my cheek and stroked it softly. I closed my eyes. Only the sudden sharp intake of my breath could have told him of the effect of that light touch.

He bent his head. I caught the scents of mint and smoke and my own secrets as his mouth moved close to mine.

I tipped my head back and opened my lips.

How long I had resisted those kisses! Now I craved his mouth, wanting to savor and prolong every sensation that could melt away my frozen, imprisoning armor of misery and isolation.

He barely grazed my lips with his.

Then he pulled himself to his knees and gently coaxed me into the same position, facing him.

Keeping his lips lightly on mine, he reached out and took my shoulders gently to bring me closer. My breasts brushed his chest with every long, shivering breath I took.

"You are free now," whispered my husband at last, releasing me, "to do as you like. . . . How will you use your liberty?"

For an answer, I put my arms around his neck, sank back upon the pillows, pulling him down to me, and brought my wild mouth to his. . . .

"Why not? In a couple of days you'll go back to Brennan Manor, and I'll go on with what I have to do, because I'm bound to do it and it isn't in me to be a deserter, no matter the reason. You have to stay near home because it's the only way you're going to know what happened to Joey, and you'll want to be there when he comes home, God willing. Who knows what will happen when all this is over? In the meantime I've found you again, and I need to tell you I love you, Audra. I never stopped loving you and I probably never will."

Audra held back tears. Why was he saying this now, when it was impossible for them to be together? Everything had changed. They were not the same people as they'd been that summer at Maple Shadows, and besides that, it was wrong to be sitting here half-undressed in front of the man she'd slept with while married to someone else, wasn't it? It was wrong to care this much about a Yankee. *All* of this was wrong, but then, what was right anymore?

He set the flask down on the table. "This might really be it, Audra; the end for you and me. But we have tonight."

"Why is it always that way for us? It was like that at Maple Shadows, and that one night you came to visit. All we ever have is one night, Lee, never knowing what will come tomorrow. I can't do that again. It hurts too much, and it's wrong."

Audra looked away as Lee began to undress. "Please take me somewhere, Lee, anywhere away from here."

He came over to kneel in front of her, grasping her wrists. "There *is* no place to take you, not tonight. And it's *not* wrong, Audra. It was *never* wrong, and you know it. And this time it isn't just tonight. When this is over, I'm coming back, and we're going to be together, do you hear me? I'm not going to live like this the rest of my life. I want you, Audra, and dammit, you want *me*! We've both known it since that first day you came here to see me, widow or not! Maybe this *is* the last chance we'll have to be together, but as God is my witness, if I don't get killed or so badly wounded that I can't come to you, I'll be back to find you, and we're going to put this war behind us!"

She looked at him pleadingly. "That's impossible now," she said in a near whisper.

myself. He doesn't know you're in here, and I don't want him to know just yet." He threw a bundle of clothes on the small table on which the lamp was sitting. "I looted those out of a clothing store like a common thief. I don't know your size. I just took a guess. You've got to have something to wear when you leave here."

Lee removed his jacket and boots, then began unbuttoning his shirt. "It's a madhouse out there. Most of the men have chased the rebels back into the countryside, and they're looting through town like crazy men. It's practically impossible to keep any of these men in line. They aren't regular army, just civilian volunteers, for the most part, come here to teach the rebels a lesson. They don't know a damn thing about real military conduct or how to obey orders." He glanced at her. "I still intend to have the bastards who attacked you whipped. How do you feel?"

She sat down on the cot, suddenly self-conscious now that she was more rested. She had removed her shoes and stockings and wore only his shirt and her bloomers. "Just terribly tired and . . . I don't know . . . numb, I guess. It's all so ugly and unreal."

"That's war, Audra, ugly and unreal. You asked me once what it's like. Now you know." He peeled off his bloodstained shirt, and Audra found herself studying his muscular arms and the familiar broad chest, the dark hair that lightly dusted that chest and led downward in a V shape past the belt of his pants. He walked to the stand that still held a bowl of water and he poured some fresh water into it, then wet a rag and held it to the cut on his arm, which was already scabbing over. "Some rebel tried to stab me with his bayonet. Missed what he was aiming for by a long shot, but he didn't miss me all together, obviously."

"Let me help you."

"Don't worry about it. It isn't bleeding anymore." He washed his face and neck, then dried off and picked up a flask of whiskey. He opened it and poured some over the cut, grimacing at the sting of it. Then he swallowed some of the whiskey straight from the flask. "They say whiskey is supposed to help ease pain," he said then. "It does, but only physical pain. It doesn't do a thing for the pain in a man's heart."

She looked away. "Lee, don't—"

TENDER BETRAYAL
by
ROSANNE BITTNER

Bestselling author of OUTLAW HEARTS
and THUNDER ON THE PLAINS

"Bittner's characters are so finely drawn, their lives so
richly detailed, one cannot help but to care deeply for
each of them." —*Affaire de Coeur*

*When Audra Brennan savored her first, forbidden taste of
desire in the arms of handsome lawyer Lee Jeffreys, his
caresses sparked a flame within that burned away the differences between rebel and Yankee.*

The shelling from the bigger guns seemed to have
stopped. She decided that at least until daylight she had no
choice but to stay here as Lee had directed. She went back
to the cot and lay down, breathing his scent on his pillow
and sheets. How odd that she felt so safe in this bed where
a Yankee soldier slept. She was in the center of the enemy
camp, yet she was not afraid.

She drifted off to sleep, losing all track of time. Finally
someone knocked gently on the rear door. "Audra? It's
me."

Audra rubbed at her eyes, holding the shirt around
herself as she found her way to the door. It was still dark.
"Lee?"

"Let me in. The worst is over."

Audra obeyed, and Lee turned and latched the door
again. Audra looked up at him, seeing blood on his right
arm. "You're hurt!"

"Nothing drastic. I told my commander I'd tend to it

he never could resist a flutter of those pretty little lashes of yours."

Sabrina's gaze shot to his face. Morgan had never given her any indication that he'd noticed her lashes before. "Even Papa was adamant this time." A soft chuckle escaped her. "It seems your reputations preceded you. He was terrified one of you might hit me over the head and drag me off by my hair."

Morgan was silent for so long that she feared she'd offended him again. Then he reached down and lifted a skein of her hair in his uninjured hand, rubbing it between thumb and forefinger. A dreamy languor stole across her features. The cadence of Sabrina's heartbeat shifted in warning.

He let the stolen tendril ripple through his fingers in a cascade of midnight silk before turning the dusky heat of his gaze on her. "I can't say I blame him, lass. If you were mine, I'd probably lock you away, too."

If you were mine . . .

The words hung suspended between them, far more awkward than their silence. In a breath of utter lunacy, Sabrina wondered how it would feel to belong to a man like him, dared to ponder what came after being dragged off by her hair.

Caught in the same spell of moonlight and solitude, Morgan's gaze dropped to her parted lips. His starving senses reeled, intoxicated by the scent of roses that flared his nostrils, the cling of her hair against his callused knuckles. He'd long ago resigned himself to the harsh life of a Highland warrior. But this girl's softness awakened old hungers and weakened his resolve. He hadn't touched a drop of wine, yet he felt drunk, reckless. What harm could one kiss to? Resisting the temptation to plunge his tongue between her unwitting lips, he leaned down and touched his mouth to hers.

At the press of Morgan's lips against her own, Sabrina's eyes fluttered shut. His kiss was brief, dry, almost tentative, yet a melting sweetness unfolded within her. She felt the leashed power in his touch. Such gentleness in a man his size wove a spell all its own. Only in the last brief second of contact did he allow himself the wicked luxury of dragging his lips across hers, molding her beneath him in perfect harmony.

Don't miss these fabulous Bantam women's fiction titles Now on sale

OFFICIAL RULES

To enter the sweepstakes below carefully follow all instructions found elsewhere in this offer.

The **Winners Classic** will award prizes with the following approximate maximum values: 1 Grand Prize: $26,500 (or $25,000 cash alternate); 1 First Prize: $3,000; 5 Second Prizes: $400 each; 35 Third Prizes: $100 each; 1,000 Fourth Prizes: $7.50 each. Total maximum retail value of Winners Classic Sweepstakes is $42,500. Some presentations of this sweepstakes may contain individual entry numbers corresponding to one or more of the aforementioned prize levels. To determine the Winners, individual entry numbers will first be compared with the winning numbers preselected by computer. For winning numbers not returned, prizes will be awarded in random drawings from among all eligible entries received. Prize choices may be offered at various levels. If a winner chooses an automobile prize, all license and registration fees, taxes, destination charges and, other expenses not offered herein are the responsibility of the winner. If a winner chooses a trip, travel must be complete within one year from the time the prize is awarded. Minors must be accompanied by an adult. Travel companion(s) must also sign release of liability. Trips are subject to space and departure availability. Certain black-out dates may apply.

The following applies to the sweepstakes named above:

No purchase necessary. You can also enter the sweepstakes by sending your name and address to: P.O. Box 508, Gibbstown, N.J. 08027. Mail each entry separately. Sweepstakes begins 6/1/93. Entries must be received by 12/30/94. Not responsible for lost, late, damaged, misdirected, illegible or postage due mail. Mechanically reproduced entries are not eligible. All entries become property of the sponsor and will not be returned.

Prize Selection/Validations: Selection of winners will be conducted no later than 5:00 PM on January 28, 1995, by an independent judging organization whose decisions are final. Random drawings will be held at 1211 Avenue of the Americas, New York, N.Y. 10036. Entrants need not be present to win. Odds of winning are determined by total number of entries received. Circulation of this sweepstakes is estimated not to exceed 200 million. All prizes are guaranteed to be awarded and delivered to winners. Winners will be notified by mail and may be required to complete an affidavit of eligibility and release of liability which must be returned within 14 days of date on notification or alternate winners will be selected in a random drawing. Any prize notification letter or any prize returned to a participating sponsor, Bantam Doubleday Dell Publishing Group, Inc., its participating divisions or subsidiaries, or the independent judging organization as undeliverable will be awarded to an alternate winner. Prizes are not transferable. No substitution for prizes except as offered or as may be necessary due to unavailability, in which case a prize of equal or greater value will be awarded. Prizes will be awarded approximately 90 days after the drawing. All taxes are the sole responsibility of the winners. Entry constitutes permission (except where prohibited by law) to use winners' names, hometowns, and likenesses for publicity purposes without further or other compensation. Prizes won by minors will be awarded in the name of parent or legal guardian.

Participation: Sweepstakes open to residents of the United States and Canada, except for the province of Quebec. Sweepstakes sponsored by Bantam Doubleday Dell Publishing Group, Inc., (BDD), 1540 Broadway, New York, NY 10036. Versions of this sweepstakes with different graphics and prize choices will be offered in conjunction with various solicitations or promotions by different subsidiaries and divisions of BDD. Where applicable, winners will have their choice of any prize offered at level won. Employees of BDD, its divisions, subsidiaries, advertising agencies, independent judging organization, and their immediate family members are not eligible.

Canadian residents, in order to win, must first correctly answer a time limited arithmetical skill testing question. Void in Puerto Rico, Quebec and wherever prohibited or restricted by law. Subject to all federal, state, local and provincial laws and regulations. For a list of major prize winners (available after 1/29/95): send a self-addressed, stamped envelope entirely separate from your entry to: Sweepstakes Winners, P.O. Box 517, Gibbstown, NJ 08027. Requests must be received by 12/30/94. DO NOT SEND ANY OTHER CORRESPONDENCE TO THIS P.O. BOX.

Dee ran her hand through his hair. "Depends," she said again.

Bending his head, he told her what he wanted, then set her on her feet and stepped back.

She raised her brows, tilted her chin, and said, "Matthew!"

He laughed and gathered her close. "Don't let them fool you, kid. Duchesses do."